The GIANT from the FIRE SEA

JOHN HIMMELMAN

ILLUSTRATED BY
JEFF HIMMELMAN

HENRY HOLT AND COMPANY • NEW YORK

Henry Holt and Company, *Publishers since 1866*
Henry Holt® is a registered trademark of Macmillan Publishing Group, LLC
175 Fifth Avenue, New York, New York 10010 • mackids.com

Library of Congress Cataloging-in-Publication Data
Names: Himmelman, John, author. | Himmelman, Jeff (Jeffrey), illustrator.
Title: The giant from the Fire Sea / John Himmelman ; illustrated by Jeff Himmelman.
Description: First edition. | New York : Henry Holt and Company, 2019. | Summary:
When a giant named Newton emerges from the Fire Sea, where Jat is gathering coal, they
begin a friendship and an adventure in which both try to protect Jat's village.
Identifiers: LCCN 2018038758 | ISBN 9781250196507 (hardcover)
Subjects: | CYAC: Giants—Fiction. | Friendship—Fiction. | Adventure and
adventurers—Fiction. | Bullying—Fiction.
Classification: LCC PZ7.H5686 Gi 2019 | DDC [Fic]—dc23
LC record available at https://lccn.loc.gov/2018038758

Our books may be purchased in bulk for promotional, educational, or business use. Please
contact your local bookseller or the Macmillan Corporate and Premium Sales Department at
(800) 221-7945 ext. 5442 or by email at MacmillanSpecialMarkets@macmillan.com.

First edition, 2019 / Designed by Carol Ly
Printed in the United States of America by LSC Communications,
Harrisonburg, Virginia

1 3 5 7 9 10 8 6 4 2

For my son, Jeff, whose *drrawings*
breathed life into a giant's land

· ONE ·
A Boy in the Flames

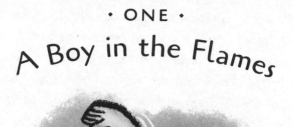

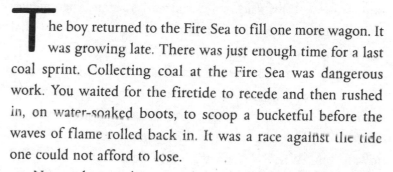

The boy returned to the Fire Sea to fill one more wagon. It was growing late. There was just enough time for a last coal sprint. Collecting coal at the Fire Sea was dangerous work. You waited for the firetide to recede and then rushed in, on water-soaked boots, to scoop a bucketful before the waves of flame rolled back in. It was a race against the tide one could not afford to lose.

No one knew what caused the sea to burn. It just did, for as far back as anyone could remember. Some said it was fed by a deep volcano. Others believed it was wizards' work. Most, however, chose not to question how and why. It was there before they were born, and it would be there long after they were gone.

The boy's day was spent darting back and forth between the advance and retreat of the blazing waves. The key to survival lay in his timing. He counted aloud his breaths between each wave. If it was ten breaths, he would use three to run in, one to scoop, and five to get out. That left one extra breath in reserve should the waves break their pattern, as they often did. A slight shift of breeze felt on the face—the only part of him exposed to the elements—was cause to abandon the scoop to wait for the current's next sequence. It would take between forty and sixty trips with his bucket to gather enough coal to fill his wagon. The heat was nearly unbearable, but he had grown used to it—as used to it as a boy could grow and not be turned to ash.

The wagon was nearly filled. "One more run. One more scoop," he said, studying the waves. "Then home, eat, sleep. Home, eat, sleeeep . . ." The boy stepped into his bucket of water to resoak his thick-soled leather boots and then moved to the edge of the simmering tide. He held the empty coal bucket tightly in his gloved hands, his body coiled, ready to charge forward. Sweat poured down his face, leaving pale streaks in the dark gray ash that coated every inch of him. The flames rolled away. He counted his breaths: "One . . . two . . . three . . ." On "nine," the tide changed direction and came toward him. When it reached his feet and receded, he would chase it in. With the back of his dirty sleeve, he cleared the sweat from his eyes and got ready to run. Then he paused, his gaze fixed on the horizon. Something broke the surface of the burning sea. It drifted slowly toward the shore. The boy stood frozen in place, squinting to focus through the heat shimmer. The firetide rolled forward and retreated a dozen times, two dozen times, and a dozen more as that drifting thing became a head, then a head upon shoulders. The boy laid down his bucket and watched as the thing, a massive, manlike thing, advanced. By the time his boots had dried, it was large enough to blot out the sun and swallow him in shadow.

He ran. There was no place to hide on the open expanse of sand, so he put some distance between them and crouched low, just short of the wooded edge behind him.

The monster from the sea watched the little creature scuttling away from him. It held up a hand the size of a rowboat.

"Do not run," it said hoarsely, its throat parched from a long stretch of breathing in fire. "Please . . ."

The boy stood up slowly but kept his distance.

"Go away!" he shouted, waving his arms. The monster stumbled forward. The boy moved closer to the woods.

"NO! GO AWAY!" repeated the boy. He turned and took a few more steps back.

"Please don't run," said the monster.

The boy stopped again.

The monster held up his hands. "Please . . . don't . . ."

"You can talk? What are you?"

"Newton," answered the monster. "Where am I?"

Newton had never seen such a small giant. It was barely as long as his foot. It couldn't be a giantling infant; it could speak, and run. And its body was too spindly for a giantling. *What a tiny nose and ears, such tiny ears. How can it hear this giant's words?* A matted tussock of black hair hung from its head. It was sooty all over from the ash of the burning sea, much like he was. Was it some kind of large bug? No. It spoke words. And wore clothes. Bugs don't speak words and wear clothes. *Maybe bugs here do.* He sniffed. *Its blood smells like a giant's; but also it does not.*

"I don't know. It's just *here*. What's a Newton?"

"A Newton is this giant. A giant of that name. I come from a far place. My boots have wandered a great long time, I am of a thought. You do not know where this *here* is?"

"I know. It's *here*. By the Fire Sea. It's home—where I live. A giant? You're a *real* giant?" The boy took a couple of cautious steps toward him. "Giants are real?"

"This one is. Others too," said Newton.

"I mean, I see that . . . But you're a giant! That talks! I thought giants were just . . . monsters in nannytales."

"This giant is real. We are real," said Newton. He crashed down to the sand. He'd been walking for weeks, or maybe years, or just days. He couldn't tell anymore. "This giant is also lost. There is no name this land is called?"

"I don't know. It's just home." The boy moved closer to Newton. "Should I be afraid of you?" he asked.

The giant let go an amused huff. "No," he answered. "Should I be afraid of *you*?"

The boy looked up at him, as if trying to read the truth in his answer. "Probably not," he said. He paused a moment, studying Newton. "Of course you would say I shouldn't be afraid of you if I should be."

"That would be lying."

"And giants don't lie? Is what you are saying?"

"No. They do. But this one doesn't. Much."

"How big are you?"

"I do not know. Did you not just see?" The giant strained to lift his hand above his head. "This big?" His arm crashed back down to the ground. "What are you?"

"Jat. A boy . . . um, man. A human."

"You are a Jataboyummanahuman?" asked Newton. "A long name to leave a mouth."

"No. Just Jat. I'm a man, or will be . . . soon. We all are here. Except for the animals. And trees. And girls. And other things that aren't any of those."

"Animals? Have you oxes? Or goats?"

"I don't," said Jat. He pointed to a hilltop in the distance. "Mr. Willowhock has cows. That's kind of an ox, I think."

Newton's eyes lit up. "*Haroomph* . . . Ox cows? Food has not fallen into this belly for so long a time. My insides roar for a fat ox cow!"

Newton slowly stood up. He was as tall as the trees that lined the edge of the beach. The giant could barely stay on his feet. His insides still buzzed with the torment he'd survived back home. The pain threatened to crumple his weakened body down to the sand. Everything was shifting, fading in and out. *This giant has splashed into the Great Sea and walked out the other side! This will not be where his boots stop carrying him!*

Food. He needed to eat. He stumbled forward toward the hilltop. *Ox cows,* he thought. He could smell them already. Drool spilled over his lower lip, leaving puddles in the sand.

The giant made it to the ranch in short time. And there they were . . . cows . . . a herd of them—all thoughtfully corralled for an easy meal. He bent down and scooped one up. *Even their ox cows are of a small size.*

"It is my regret, ox cow," he said, and shoved it into his mouth and swallowed. "Thank you, ox cow." He picked up another. "It is my regret, ox cow." That one followed the first. "Thank you, ox cow." Soon he'd finished off the herd, thanking each after it had been dropped down his cavernous gullet. Jat caught up to him, out of breath. He seemed to have overcome his fear of the giant. Newton was sitting against a tree, eyes closed. A satisfied smile stretched beneath a nose larger than three full sacks of potatoes.

"What did you do?" he shouted.

"Ate," said Newton. He patted his massive belly. "This giant feels better now."

"Mr. Willowhock will not feel better when he sees you ate all of his cows!" Then he took a step back. "You're not still hungry, are you?"

"Always still hungry," said Newton.

"Am I something that would make you *less* hungry?"

"*Haroomph*, this giant has told you not to fear him. You are of a giant's smell, in a small way, but enough of a way for this giant not to make you food. We do not eat each other, big or small." Newton gave him another sniff. *He does not smell like a bad thing to eat, though.* His stomach rumbled. *NO! If it speaks it is not to eat!*

"Then let's go," said Jat. "Mr. Willowhock can always find ways to make trouble for . . . people. I shouldn't have told you about his cows."

"But it is a thing that makes this giant grateful to you."

"I didn't know this would happen."

Newton was confused. "When giants are hungry, giants eat. It all becomes the same."

"The same? What's *the same*?"

"I eat your ox. You eat my goat. She eats his swan. He gives his ax. We all take. We all give. We all *eat*. It is *take-give*."

"But you didn't give him anything for his cows," said Jat. "And you have to ask first, to make sure you both agree." The boy paused. "Unless you're a giant and can crush anyone you want, I guess. Which you are and probably can."

"This giant does not wish to crush mans. A time will come when I make the balance," said the giant. "It is how it works."

"Okay," said the boy, "but until then, you really have to go! Mr. Willowhock is a nasty old croak. He will be so mad he will *make* you crush him to stop him."

Newton stood and let out a great belch, blowing a treeful of grackles from their perches. He did feel a little better, although the pain inside him still crashed around like an angry bull. He allowed it the freedom to run through him. It was easier than fighting it. *Play with the little ox cows I gave you,* he said silently to the turmoil within. The giant left the ranch and stomped back toward the fireshore. Seeing where he came from might help him figure out where he was and where he might go from here.

"There is a cave not very far," said Jat, running to keep up. "Giants live in caves, right? At least the ones in stories do. Maybe you can stay there until you figure out what you are doing. What *are* you doing? Where did you come from? Why are you here?"

"Do all of you mans talk so fast?"

"No. I don't know. It's just . . . I just saw a giant shove a herd of cows in its mouth. I don't see that a lot. I don't think I want to ever see it again. Are more of you coming?"

"This giant hopes not. I am not much loved where I came from. There are stories to tell, man . . . human-jat-boy."

"Just Jat."

Newton looked down at the boy and smiled. "You are not of a fear anymore?"

Jat stepped back, his eyes wide in panic. "Why? What are you going to do . . . ?"

Newton shook his head in frustration. He got down on a knee. The boy backed away farther.

"What this giant will do is ask the boy-jat—"

"Just Jat."

"He will ask the just-jat to trust that when this giant says a thing, his words hide no lies. I have known fear from giants all of my days. It is why I am here. Because I have known it, I do not wish to bring it to others. Please know . . . this . . . giant . . . will . . . not . . . hurt . . . you."

Jat's face relaxed again. "I believe you. But there's a word I'm thinking of—*porridge* . . . No . . . *potten. Potential!* It's something that can happen. You have to understand that when I see you, I can see *potential* of a great big monster . . . just squashing me. I couldn't stop you."

"There is porridge that you can hurt me, too," said Newton, "and yet this giant is of no fear of it."

"Yeeeaahhh . . . but really no. And not the right word. There's just more reasons not to trust people than to trust them. I think I trust you, though. Aside from running away and hiding, I don't think there's much choice *but* to trust you."

"*Hoomph!*" said the giant. He got back to his feet. "I am not of a wish to keep speaking of eating and squashing just-jats. This giant is in a new land he knows nothing about. That is a thing of great interest to me now."

"The cave is up ahead, in the side of that cliff. You'll find it," said Jat. "I really have to get home now." He sighed. "There are men waiting back home for those coals in my wagon. I know for sure my mother is already thinking of ways to make me sorry I'm so late. Will you be here tomorrow? Please don't go anywhere yet."

"Will you tell me more about where I am?" asked Newton. "I am thinking this is my land now, too. My *just here*. For a time, at least. I should learn about it."

"Are you joking? Do giants joke? Of course I'll be back. I'll tell you all about this place! I mean, you're a rippin' giant! The only way I won't be back is if I wake up tomorrow and this was just a dream."

"I will not leave here without seeing you tomorrow, just-jat."

"Jat."

"Jat," said the giant.

The boy retrieved his cart and disappeared down the sandy trail that opened up at the edge of the woods. Newton found the cave. It was tall enough for him to stand inside and deep enough to allow him to lie down, but unlike what the boy believed, most giants didn't live in caves. Newton was one of those who did not. His body could feel the weight of the rock above and around him, and it was almost too much to bear. He chose instead to lean up against the wall outside so he could study the stars. They were the first he had seen since he'd entered the sea of fire. He was surprised to see they looked the same as in his own land, except all shifted over to a different part of the sky. *"I thought you were just monsters in nannytales,"* the boy had said. *Fum,* thought the giant. *He has heard of giants, but he did not think we are real. He has heard of giants, and we are real. Am I not the first to travel to this land?* Newton knew that *giant* meant large, but he never understood why they would call themselves large. *Large compared to what?* he wondered. *Compared to mans? Did* they *name us?*

He had so many questions for the mans-boy—Jat. Newton absently picked up a stone from the sand and rolled it around in his fingers. It left a dry red powder on his hand, and he wiped it off on the rock wall behind him. The giant stared at the long smear on the surface. He turned and scraped the stone against the wall. *This is better than scratching sticks into bark!*

Newton stood and drew an image of a giant. It looked like him, or what he thought he looked like. He made it as tall as he was. Back home he had done a similar thing, but instead they were lines pricked on small sheets of pale bark. This felt different. It was big, like he was, and looked back at him, eye to eye. He added the Fire Sea and then some ox cows. He had been thinking how good they tasted and drew them in his belly. The giant stepped back and looked at what he had done. A feeling came over him he had never felt before. *I have made another Newton*, he thought, *and I have fed his hungry belly. Do the holy-giants know of this magic?* He patted his own stomach. He would be hungry again soon, but he was always hungry again soon.

Newton lifted his shirt and, with the red stone, scrawled an ox cow onto his belly. He closed his eyes, trying to feel if this filled him. It might have, a little. He wasn't sure. He would need to find real food again. The rules were different here. *You cannot take and promise to give? What kind of land is this?*

Newton sat back down against the wall and gazed out at the Fire Sea. Fire was a giant's friend, usually. Flame was soothing to the skin. Unfortunately, it could also quickly devour that which a giant held most dear.

TWO

The Willowhock

Abner Willowhock returned in the morning with a wagonful of corn for his cows. The corn would fatten them up for slaughter in a few weeks. The purchase dug into his savings, but his livestock would fetch him a heavy sack of coppers. It would bring in enough to get him through winter, and maybe into spring, with a little left to squander. While Willowhock claimed they were *his* cows, in truth, more than half were not, at least originally. Six had come from his nephew, who stole them from another ranch. Their brands, a letter *O* on their left flank, revealed them to be the property of Silas Otis of Flinders Gorge, a two days' ride west. Abner seared his *W* in the middle of the *O*s, and then branded *O*s around the *W*s on the rest of his cows. When he was done, they all appeared to belong to the same owner.

"They all be mine now," he cackled proudly. "And who's ta say different?"

But now the cows were gone—his *and* Otis's. The fences he'd built to pen them in destroyed, ground into the dirt. He searched the area but found nothing but a few dead birds scattered around the old maple.

"Who did this?" he shouted. The woods were silent. Willowhock ran into his barn and returned with his hatchet.

"I'll find yeh and deal with yeh myself," he muttered. Then he shouted to the sky, "I *will* find yeh, thiefs!" He circled the pen, searching for footprints, widening his coverage with each round. "I know there be more than one of yeh. Tracks. Tracksy tracks . . . Tracksy tracksy tracks . . . Where be your filthy stealin', fence-crushin' tracksy tracks?"

The rancher tripped over a clod of dirt. He stood up and took a step back. A ridge of mud surrounded him. He hopped out of the depression and walked around its edge.

"A footprint, maybe? Well, yeh be a big one. A mighty big one, if that's what it be!" He paced out the print. Four and a half steps. "So, yeh found a big friend ta take yeh cows back, eh, Otis?" He shook his ax in the air. "No matter. I can chop down a tree, I can chop down yeh big thiefin' friend!"

Willowhock searched for another footprint. Then he saw an opening in the thin patch of woods that surrounded his ranch. It was lined with mangled trees leading to the shore of the Fire Sea. The clearing had not been there when he'd left the day before.

"So that's where yeh went, thiefs."

The rancher looked down again at the huge footprint. He ran back to the barn and returned with a bigger ax. The giant's trail was easy to follow, and in good time he stood before his rustler.

"Ho there, thief," he called up to the giant. "Bigger'n I thought," he said under his breath.

Newton awoke and sat up. He looked down at the angry farmer, now the second mans he'd come across. This one was slightly taller than the boy, although a bit more bent. His clothes were faded black and covered in dust. Newton bent forward and tried to see his face, but it was hidden in shadow beneath a floppy, wide-brimmed hat. The giant's attention shifted to the long-handled ax held threateningly in his bony hands.

"Ho there, thief," Newton greeted him. "You are another mans, yes?"

"What be a giant doing here when there's no such thing as yeh?" asked Willowhock.

"I left my home from across there," he said, pointing to the sea. "There was danger for me I chose not to greet. I am Newton."

"There be danger for yeh here, too. I want my cows."

"Oh . . . You grew those little ox cows? Thank you for them. I do not know yet what I will give you for them. It will be something good. Something very good." Newton smiled. Giants took great pride in their take-give.

"You will give me my cows back," said the man. "I don't care what manner of magical beast you are!"

"Magical beast? *Fum.* Not this giant. Just a hungry one." The giant patted his belly. "And I do not think you want them now." He laughed. "Do not worry. A boy-mans told me that you do not take-give. I will not do it again. Your ox cows will be made to balance when I have a balance to give. Would you have more, maybe?"

"What manner a' rat-spittle are ye sprayin' in me face? Give me my cows!" Willowhock took a step forward and raised his ax.

"It is wrong for the giver to demand his balance," scolded Newton. "I do not know your ways yet, but I do know mine, which is all this giant has. Your balance will come, but you must not ask! If you demand it, you will not get it! It is how it works."

"Yeh not be in yeh giant land anymore. Yeh be in Willowhock land. If yeh take it, yeh pay when I say yeh pay!"

Newton picked up a handful of boulders and dropped them in front of the man. Willowhock jumped away.

"Here is your balance," said the giant. "Accept it, or do not. It is all that I have. I cannot give you back your ox cows."

"Then down come the tree!" Willowhock charged forward and struck Newton in the ankle with his ax. The ax bounced harmlessly off the giant's tough hide and hit Willowhock in his forehead. The man fell to the sand. He stood up, rubbing his bloodied head, and bent down to retrieve his ax. In a fit of rage, he threw it at Newton. The ax spun through the air, hit him in the back of his hand, and again bounced off. Newton picked it up and held it to his face to study it more closely.

"Do mans use these little axes for battle? We giants do, too, but they are of a more bigger size." He handed the ax back to Willowhock. The farmer hesitated a moment and then snatched it from his fingers.

"It is my regret I do not know your Willowhock laws. It is my regret I ate your ox cows. You gave me your ax, and I return it. Let us be as friends now."

Abner Willowhock huffed and stormed back up the beach.

"I will have my cows, thief," he spat over his shoulder.

THREE

Gooses and Muddleducks

J at had arrived home very late the night before. The buyers for his firecoal were long gone. His mother was incensed.

"*Three* waited for you. *Three* left with NO coal for them and NO coppers for us!"

"I'm sorry," said Jat.

"If you are going to risk your life doing this, *despite* that I don't want you to, you should at least not be doing it for nothing! Where were you? You were *not* running the tides in the dark, were you?"

"No, I . . . got to talking to someone. He is new to . . . here. I lost track of time. I'm sorry. Will they be back? Can I go to them now?"

His mother glared at him. "You have to be honest with me, Jat. I mean it! Were they after you again?" She reached out and lifted his hair from his face, searching for bruises or scrapes. "I swear, I will knock them all out! I don't care who their mother is!"

Jat pushed her hand away. "Please stop. It wasn't them. And you couldn't knock them out if it was. I told you, I was talking to someone, and it got late. I'm sorry, okay?"

"Who were you talking to?"

"A . . . man. He was lost. We were just talking. I told him where he could find . . . a bite to eat."

"I don't like it. Don't you have enough problems of your own without you helping strange men?"

"Who said he was strange? *Although* . . . Mother, I'm all right! And I have the coal. I can bring it to them now. I'm not tired, too much . . ."

Her features slowly softened. "No, Jat," she said. "I don't want you bumping around in the dark with a cart full of coal. They are coming back in the morning. But we will have to take less for the firecoal. For the two trips they had to make."

"But I can't . . . I won't be here in the morning!"

"Why not?"

"I can't say yet."

"Then you'll be here in the morning," she said. "If I was strong enough to shovel it into their carts, I would, Jat." She held out her arms. A return hug was part of his mother's ritual since the death of his father. This one lasted longer than usual.

"Okay," said Jat finally. "Are you okay?"

"Yes," said his mother. "Now that I know you are. Jat . . . I was mostly angry because I was worried. We can't do this anymore—have you risk your life like this. If your sister wasn't here, I'd have gone looking for you. I almost brought her with me. We are going to find another way. Every time you leave, I dread that what happened to . . . And tonight, you came home so late . . . I—" She broke off and turned her face away from her son. This was an old conversation. And it was one that surfaced more and more frequently. Neither could come up with a solution that did not involve them moving away. But to where? And then what? Jat took his mother's hand.

"You know how careful I am," he said. "And fast! Besides, I had an idea on my way home. I need to give it some more thought, but . . . I'm starving. Did you save me some dinner?"

Late the next morning, the three men, still grumpy at being stood up the night before, left with their sacks of firecoal.

"Going!" shouted Jat to his mother, and he flew down the trail that led to the shore. Without the coalcart slowing him down, he was able to reach it in half the time it normally took. He raced to the cave where he'd sent the giant the night before. Newton was still there, deeply engrossed in covering the rock wall with drawings.

"It's you!" said the boy, looking at the artwork. "And the Fire Sea. And more giants. Are they your friends?"

"One, yes," said Newton. "The others, no. I was thinking about my home. It was not a place of great peace for this giant. But it was what this giant knew. Home. We know our home."

Jat looked away a moment, and then back at Newton.

"This isn't always a *place of great peace* for . . . everyone, either. It's home for me, but I wish it wasn't. You should do good here, though."

"Are things bad for you, Jat-boy?"

"Jat. No. They're fine. Are you going back?"

"*Haroomph* . . . I can never go back."

"Can't you just go back the way you came? Not that I'm saying I want you to."

"No," said the giant. He traced his finger along his drawing. "Do you see where I made the Fire Sea? It comes to an end here, at a place of turning water at the edge of the Great Sea. Across that water, where I made these giants, here, is my home."

"Then you can walk back to it through the fire and swim home when you get to the water."

Newton smiled, then shook his head. "Giants cannot swim."

"I can teach you," said Jat. "But really, not that I want you to go."

"What would happen if you sank? Would you not turn to stone?"

"Never heard of *that*. You turn to stone in water?"

"It is not the water," said Newton. "Giants turn to stone when they are taken by a strong fear. Mans do not?"

"No."

"What happens to you?"

"I don't know. We run. Or hide. Usually we shake a bit."

"Mans are small, but brave to not turn! We turn for a short time. And then we turn back, except when . . . when we do not." A sadness crossed the giant's great face. *Two did not,* he thought. He looked away, across the Fire Sea. *Why do they enter my head now?* He huffed through his nose. *Because* home. Home was where his family was. His parents—the two who *did not turn back*. He had traveled over an ocean of water and an ocean of fire, but back across that great farness, his parents still sat in *Everstone*. The distance did not ease the shame-burden that slept inside him, so easily awakened. Newton turned back to Jat. They were talking about crossing oceans.

"Water," he said. "One fear that lives in all giants is that when we sink, we will stay sinked. We cannot breathe in water, and we would not rise to see the sun again. The fear of this turns us to stone."

"And turning to stone makes the fear come true. You are stuck, aren't you? You're afraid a real thing is going to happen, and the real thing happens because you are afraid."

Newton thought about this. "Yes, Jat. This is of an odd truth. It seems that if half of it is made to go away, the *whole* trouble will follow." Newton had been working on controlling his *turning*. He was growing better at it—better than most giants. The secret, although he didn't realize it, was to care less about what happened to you. This mans gave him a curious new way to look at the problem.

"This giant did find a way for his boots to travel the sea, though. I tied a bundle of cobbletrees together and let them carry me. They do not sink, and I do not know why. They are of a greater weight than this giant, who *would* sink. A magic of a kind, maybe? But again, maybe no. Too often we call magic things we just do not understand . . . But when the trees reached your sea of fire, they burned. I fell to the bottom and walked here."

"So you can really breathe in fire? I know what I saw, but it's still hard to believe."

"Yes. Mans cannot?"

"No. Not at all. No fire. No water. Just air."

"Just air," said Newton. "Just air is best for giants, too."

"Who is that big giant?" asked the boy, pointing at the wall.

"That is my friend Pryat. He is big and strong. He likes to fight. Do you see that I gave him a smile to wear?"

"That's a big smile," said the boy.

"Yes. I want him to be happy on the wall. He was not happy when I saw him last. Pryat put himself in danger to save this giant's hide. *Haroomph* . . . Yes, this giant's hide was in danger because Pryat was an oaf, but an oaf can be an oaf and still have a giant make him smile on a wall."

"How about your mother? Or your father? Do they look like you?"

Newton turned his head away. "That is not a thing I will speak of. It is a story that carries pain."

"I'm sorry. What's that thing with the big nose next to your friend?"

"*Foomph* . . . She is Marlite. She is a holygiant now. She is no longer a friend." Newton winced and grabbed his belly.

"What's wrong?" asked Jat.

"It is a pain. And it is of an oddness it strikes now, in front of the holygiant."

"She did this?"

"No, but she did not stop what was done." The giant wondered how much to tell the boy. *Would he understand?* Would his words bring him trouble here as they had back home? He looked at the image of Marlite. The pain was fading. *It is of a relief this Marlite on the wall does not attack the giant who made it. And a foolish thought of my own that she could.* Earlier, he had worked on her hair, added crisscrosses in the braid that snaked down to the ground. Newton had tugged on that braid when they were as giantlings, something he would not have dared once she became a holygiant.

Jat interrupted his thoughts. "Are you okay? Do you need something? A healer? We have one in our village."

"No. It has passed."

"Good. I was thinking about something. Actually a couple things, but one thing first."

"And what would be that one thing first?"

"If I brought you back to my village, would you eat our people?"

"Perhaps. Are *peoples* good to eat?" asked the giant.

"No, they're like me. It's what you call a bunch of . . . I don't know, *me*s. I know you won't eat *me*. But I want them to see you, and, well . . . again, I remember those cows."

"I would not eat your friends, or others like you . . . *peoples* or *mans*," said the giant. "We do not eat things with two legs, unless it has wings. Do some of you fly?"

"No," said Jat. "Only birds fly. You can eat those, if you want. Unless they're someone else's. Some of us raise chickens and ducks. Some raise geese. But, again, *if they're someone else's* . . ."

"Oh," said Newton. "Giants eat gooses and muddleducks, too!" He was so excited, he pulled a stone from his pocket and drew geese and ducks next to the image of himself on the wall. Then he added a few more to join the drawings of cows in his belly. "This Newton is happy," he said, pointing to his sated portrait. Then he patted his stomach. "And soon this one will be, too!"

He stopped drawing and looked down at the boy. "Oh! Your Willowhock came to me. The one with the ox cows. He is *not* happy. Look. I scratched him into the wall."

Jat gasped. "You did what to him?"

Newton frowned. "Not in that way!"

The boy studied the drawing. "He looks mad. I told you."

"HO! It is how I tried to make him—on here, the wall—not the real him. On the wall him, I made an angry mouth line . . . it is like making the happy mouth line but turning it up the downsides."

"What did he do?"

"He wants his ox cows. I told him they are gone. I told him that it is wrong to demand balance. To demand balance loses balance. It is how giants live."

Jat thought a moment. "You do remember what I told you, right? You can't just take things without an agreement first. Well, *you* can, but it's not how it's done here, unless you're a thief. We don't have a lot of those here, but some show up sometimes . . ."

"What is a thief? It is a word the Willowhock used. At first hearing I thought it to mean 'friend.' But I do not think that now."

"Thieves are people who take things from other people who don't want them to take it."

Newton's cheeks turned blue. "That is stealing!"

"Whoa! Your face is blue!"

"Taking things from other giants who don't want them to take it is stealing!"

"That's what thieves do."

"But I told him I was of a plan to make balance. This giant is no *thief*!"

"I know, I know! You told me," said Jat.

"How does a giant make not happen what has already happened?"

"You can't, I guess," said the boy. "I have a question. Is giants' blood blue?"

"Yes."

"Huh. I thought so. Your cheeks just turned blue."

Newton ignored him. "*Humph* . . . I will still make the balance. I always do and always will. Even if the asker is rude."

· FOUR ·
Newton's Peoples

The boy and the giant set off for the village. At first, the people ran in fear when they saw Newton. Soon, however, it became clear this was not a monster on the rampage. They began to tag along, clearly eager to take in an eyeful of this mountainous creature. Newton smiled at them nervously. He'd spent most of his life trying to avoid bringing attention to himself, and here he was leading a parade.

"Hey, Sootyboy! Come here," shouted a voice in the crowd. Jat ignored it.

"Who is Sootyboy?" asked Newton. "You? You have more names? Many giants have two names—the one given to us and one we choose later. Some just keep the old. This giant did not."

"Just keep going," said Jat.

Another voice chimed in. "We see you, Sootyboy. You

washed your face today, Sootyboy? We can still smell ya! Why are you hiding behind that thing?"

"Me? Am I the thing?" asked Newton. "Are those mans-boys your friends?"

Jat glowered. He kept his eyes forward. "Keep going."

"I smell fire. Someone burning?" shouted one of the boys.

Newton sniffed. "There is no fire burning." He bent down and sniffed Jat. "You do smell of the Fire Sea." The giant turned to the boys. "He is not burning. He just smells of the Fire Sea."

Laughter exploded from some in the crowd.

"Keep . . . going!" said Jat to the giant.

"Stop there!" shouted a voice. It was Constable Maurice Stoggin, or just Constable, or Stoggin, as nearly everyone called him. Stoggin had been charged by Lord and Lady Ellery to keep the peace in the township. If someone made trouble, it was his job to stop it before it became trouble for the lord and lady. He stood in the middle of the road, spear held at the ready. His three deputies lined up behind him, spears also raised. The sticklike one on the left was his son, Thumbridge. He was often referred to as "Scarecrow." However, that name was only safe to use behind his back. Thumbridge lived to follow in his father's footsteps. Laws were meant to be heeded, if not for the good of a person, then for the good of the law itself. On the other side was Budge, the baker's son. His father had made him join the constable's deputies to toughen him up. The constable didn't want him, but the boy's father was relentless in begging him take on his son. It became easier to give in than to avoid the man. Budge was often missing when he was most needed, which rarely mattered because he was rarely needed. And he was rarely needed because he was mostly useless. Newton looked down at the rosy-cheeked deputy and gave a sniff. Living above a baker's kitchen steeped the boy in the sweet aroma of fresh breads. *If I was to eat a mans, this one smells the most tasty.* The giant shook his head. *No! Mans aren't food. This giant must be very hungry!*

The girl standing in the middle was someone Jat knew but could not look in the eye, Bonnie Mullein. Most would likely notice her first, in her long, green, grasshoppery waist-coat. It had lots of hidden pockets that held lots of hidden things. Her agile frame was topped with straight black hair pulled back away from her sea-green eyes. She and Jat were about the same age, maybe a year apart, and had crossed paths a number of times before. She was always friendly to him, for some reason, one of the few his age who were. He had once asked her to the barn dance, but she declined, say-ing she was going with Durd Fengiss, the boy who had just moments ago exclaimed, "I smell fire . . ."

When his mother learned Bonnie had turned her son down, she simply said, "That's for the best. She chases trouble and always catches it." What he didn't tell her was who she was going with.

Durd and his friend had run an endless campaign of war against Jat. They mocked how he was always covered in coal-dust, which was hard to wash off. They taunted him about how he smelled like a wet fireplace. Durd's brother, Sack, a hulk of a boy, found it particularly amusing that Jat's father had died collecting coal in the Fire Sea, despite the fact that his own father had gone missing some time ago. When Jat men-tioned this in response, it got him beaten up even worse. Jat did his best to avoid them, but this was hard to do in a village so small. Beatings were a part of his life—when they could catch him. While he wasn't much of a fighter, years of chasing the tide made him a very fast sprinter.

After the dance, Durd tried to steal a kiss from Bonnie. She punched him in the stomach and made him throw up.

Unfortunately for Jat, he was there, by himself as usual, when it happened. He made the mistake of saying to Durd as he knelt on the ground wiping his chin, "You should have eaten a smaller lunch." Durd stood up, and he and Sack beat him nearly senseless, until Bonnie stepped in again. She twisted Durd's arm behind his back.

"Say you're sorry to the kid," she demanded. Sack started to step forward. Bonnie gave him a look that made him back off. "Say you're sorry," she repeated.

"Sorry!" spat Durd. Bonnie let him go. "*Kid*," he added with a smile.

"If they ever give you trouble again, you tell me," she said to Jat. "I'll handle them."

Jat winced.

"Are you hurt?" asked Bonnie.

"No! Well, yeah, but that is the worst thing you could have said!"

Bonnie frowned. "Huh . . . you're *welcome*," she snapped icily, and stomped off.

When Durd and Sack found Jat alone, they both picked up where they left off. "Where's your girlfriend, Sootyboy?" Durd asked. "Get used to this. And if you tell her, it'll be worse."

While the beatings became a part of his life, Jat never got used to them.

Bonnie had recently become an apprentice deputy, for something to do. The position also helped her get out of the "trouble she chased." The three were known in the village as "Stoggin's Boys." Bonnie was fine with that.

"What do you want with us?" the constable shouted up to Newton.

Newton looked down at Jat, who shrugged, and then back to Stoggin.

"I am here from the Great Sea. Your Jat brings me to meet his people."

"Are you a giant?" asked a voice in the crowd.

"Yes," said Newton. "How can you know what I am, when I have not heard of your kind before? *Mans* . . ."

"Well, look at ya!" someone shouted. The crowd bubbled in hushed murmurs, the words "giant" and "oh my" popping up more than any other. Added to that were varying expressions of concern about becoming its meal or getting stepped on. Constable Stoggin and his "boys" stood their ground, spears angled up toward Newton's shin.

"You are not welcome here!" yelled the constable. "Go now, or we will drive you off!"

Jat stepped forward. "He won't hurt us. He left his home and got lost. I brought him here because he is alone in our land." He added, "And look at him. Did you ever see anything like it? Him? . . . It?"

"*Him* would be more nice," said Newton.

"You brought this monster to feed on our village? Good. Let him eat you first," said Thumbridge.

"Careful calling it names," whispered Budge, his spear a blur in his shaking hands. "I think it can hear us."

Bonnie said nothing; her eyes, and spearpoint, appeared to be searching for a reachable soft spot on the giant.

"He's not going to eat us," said Jat.

"Oh, that's enough, Maurice." An old woman elbowed through the crowd. "If this thing was going to eat us, you'd be sliding down its gullet by now." She walked up to the giant, her eyes slowly scaling his great height. "Wow!" she exclaimed, and then asked, "Well? *Are* you going to eat us?"

"Why do all of you ask me that? Do a lot of things eat you?"

The old woman laughed and turned back to the constable.

"Maurice Stoggin, put your spear down. You look foolish. All of you! Bonnie, what are you doing with these boys?" The girl shrugged.

"Flora, this is not your business," said Stoggin. "I am entrusted—"

"To get us all squashed like bugs. What are you going to do with that spear? Remove a splinter from its finger?"

"His," corrected Jat.

"His what?" asked the woman.

"His, not 'its.'"

Bonnie leaned toward Flora and whispered, "I think if I get it just under its toenail, it'll go runnin' off pretty fast."

"This giant would not squash you . . . like bugs," said Newton. "I will leave."

"Oh, we won't hurt you, even if we could. PUT DOWN THAT SPEAR, Maurice! Thummy, Budge—put your spears down. Bonnie? You especially!" The constable lowered his weapon; his "boys" followed suit. Bonnie continued to stare at the toe of the giant's boot.

"Come to our circle," continued Flora. "You'll have more room to stretch out, and we would hear your story."

The giant looked down at Jat, his expression asking if he should.

"That's why I brought you here," said the boy. "I think it's okay."

"And she is your leader?" he whispered.

"Um . . . not officially, but she kind of is even though she really isn't," said Jat. "And you should know that your whispers are louder than four morning roosters."

The constable leaned in toward the old woman on their way into the village. "Please don't call me Maurice in front of people, Flora. It undermines my authority."

"Oh, stop it, Maurice. I've been calling you that since you were at your momma's breast."

"And don't say that again either, ever!"

Newton, and nearly every man, woman, and child in the small community crowded into the village circle. Newton sat down to bring his face a little closer to theirs. He took in the gathering, amazed so many would come out to meet him. The last time he was so surrounded, it was in another land across two seas. *And the smiles I see here were as frowns there.*

He answered what questions he could. When it came to why he was here, Newton found that more difficult to explain. *How much should I tell them? How much should I not tell them?* He leaned over to Jat.

"I do not know your mans ways," he whispered. "If this giant says a thing that would not be good for him, give a kick to stop him."

"Don't worry about it, Newton."

"But I am of a thought of the ox cows," he whispered. "The no *take-give*? . . . *Angry face on wall*? . . . *The Willowhock* . . ."

"I know—I know. Just tell us what you want, *if* you want," said the boy. "And we all heard you just now, anyway."

"*Fum!* Okay. A time ago," he started, "the Great Sea of my land carried to the shore a stone crate of . . . I call them *silent speakers*. I learned to hear in my head the scratches on the bark inside them, and they told me of . . . lands and stars in the night sky." Newton leaned back and looked up. It was daytime and there were only clouds above him. His silent speakers spoke little of clouds. But he had his own thoughts about them.

"This giant—*no* giant—has thought to look up at them before. Looking up is hard for us. We do not bend in that way. Giants look *down*. This giant made a . . . *farlooker* from *waterstones* to see the stars and lands of the night sky more close. But then *skyfire* filled the sky—rocks of fire, sent by the Makers' Dragon. One of them came down in our village and burned many homes. The Elder Council and holygiants say it was to punish us for my spying on the Makers in the stars. *FUM* I said, and *FUM* I say! Giants believe that all they need, all they want, all their land, all their goats and oxes, are below their noses. But this giant lifted his eyes. This giant looked up. And this giant was . . . punished . . ." Newton unconsciously hugged his ribs, feeling his punishment. He looked down at the mans. Some were beginning to look frightened.

"This giant is getting loud. It is my regret. I am not of anger at you, but at the oafish giants back home. Our Elder Council speaks for all giants. Our holygiants speak for the

Makers. *Together* they spoke that this giant was of a danger to them. I escaped on a jumble of cobbletrees tied together to float on the Great Sea." He caught himself and stopped. "I should not be speaking of this."

"It's okay," said Flora. "We know you got here somehow and for some reason. What, or where, is the Great Sea?"

"It is the water that surrounds my land. Giants do not enter it. We do not float like jumbles of cobbletrees. We sink like piles of stones. But the trees carried this giant away. At the end of the Great Sea there is a spinning water of five colors, one not a color, but . . . nothing. A color of nothing. I followed the red stream. You must know of it. Do you?"

No one did. Flora looked as if she were about to speak, but stopped. Newton continued. "It brought me to your Fire Sea, where my jumble of trees burned. I fell to the bottom and walked for . . . this giant knows not how long." He looked down at Jat, who was looking back up at him, rapt in his story. "I left your Fire Sea and met your Jat, and here this giant sits."

"What is this spinning water?" asked Garn Fleck, a fisherman. "There is no end to the Fire Sea. It has ocean on the sides, but no one can reach where it stops. It just keeps going. We can't get around it or behind it."

Newton shrugged. "This giant does not know. His boots went where the jumble of trees took them."

"Are you moving on from here?" asked Constable Stoggin. "It might be a good idea to keep going. To keep moving. On from here . . ."

"Why?" asked Jat. "He should stay here! He was already

chased away from one place—for very dumb reasons. *Because he looked in the sky?* We'd all be in trouble for that."

Newton looked back down at the boy. "Thank you."

"What will you eat?" asked a voice in the crowd.

"Eat Sootyboy!" shouted another voice. "He's already cooked!" A few laughed. Bonnie shot a look in their direction and the laughter stopped.

The giant didn't know the answer to that. He was glad the question was asked, though; he had been wondering that himself.

"HA! If you eat meat, I'll give you eight cows and a bull," said Greetas McGilvry. "*If* you dig me a new pond to water the rest of my herd."

"I got goats 'n' sheep if that's to your likin'," said Maynard Hinson. "But you need to clear a stretch of woods for a new field before you get 'em."

"How about geese? I have more than I can feed and more than I can sell," said Agnes Boone. "Fix my roof and you can eat my extras."

Newton leaned down and whispered to Jat, although, again, everyone heard him easily. "You do practice take-give."

"In a way," said Jat. "But notice it's more of a *give-take*; the 'give' is there before the 'take.'"

Villager after villager offered food in exchange for work best left for a giant. Newton was beginning to feel, for the first time in so very long a time, welcome. The mans were to be his friends now. His . . . *peoples? Is that the word? Peoples means many friends, yes?* Those who feed you become your *peoples . . .*

Day turned to evening. No one seemed eager to return to his or her home. There was little excitement in their quiet village, and the arrival of a mythical creature greatly livened things up. Lanterns were lit and moved closer to the circle. Some of the shopkeepers set up tables of food to sell to the throng. People pushed in close to the giant, eager, although somewhat hesitant, to touch him—to touch a real live giant. It made Newton a little nervous, but he thought that maybe this was a thing mans did. And a few good sniffs showed their blood to be free of bad wishes. *What smells different in their blood? There is a giantness to it, but again, there is not.*

Finally, Newton had to ask their leave. He did not feel well. Jat accompanied him to the edge of the village. A small group followed. Jat turned around. The Fengiss brothers and their friend Mason Twirp were among them.

"Let him go. He needs to rest," he shouted to them.

"Who are you to say?" asked Mason.

"His friend. Come on. Give him some room."

"This giant would be grateful," said Newton. Most of the group turned back. Jat's three tormentors lingered, exchanging whispers.

"Are you okay?" Jat asked the giant. "You really don't look good. I can see it in your face. It's like yesterday." Newton didn't hear him. The pain was returning in waves, and those waves were crashing hard against his insides. He clutched his belly and willed it to pass. *It is getting worse.*

"Newton? Did you hear me? Are you okay?"

"It is a thing I carried in me from my land," he answered.

"Yes, your *punishment*. Something is in you? What is in you? Is it an actual thing?" asked the boy.

"*Hroomph* . . . I do not know. It is the Makers' Voice. Or lightning scars. All this talk brings my thoughts back home, and I wish that you do not join me. Come see me tomorrow, Jat." The giant picked up his pace and stumbled back to the cave.

Jat was left behind. The boys who were following caught up with him.

· FIVE ·

The Makers' Voice

Back at the shore, Newton collapsed against the cliff wall beside the mouth of the cave. He rolled over and crawled partially inside, seeking the quiet of the darkness within. Sometimes darkness helped. He didn't need to go in very far. He kept his feet near the opening so he could escape if the whole thing came crashing down, like it felt it would do. Newton knew it just *felt* that way, though. It did not mean it would. He wanted something solid around him. The cave walls hugged him as a mother's arms, in that darkness. *Mother* . . . Like a wounded ridgebear, he lay on his side, knees pulled up to his chest. He was of a great hunger to go to a place that was not where he was right now. Sleep would bring him there. But too often it brought him to a *more worse* place, a place in his memory. There was once a time he did not worry where sleep would carry him. That was before the Makers' Ear.

Newton slipped off into his slumber-journey.

He was home again, walking across the village center, past where he had been kept in his cell. Gabroc, High Elder of the Elder Council, kept pace beside him. Gabroc was the smallest in the group—forty feet from the soles of his oxhide boots to the top of his hairless head. His granitey skin was just beginning to show the cracks of age. He wore the brown-green robes that typically adorned the aging bodies of the Elder Council. A dull bronze medallion hung from a vine around his neck, signifying his high status in the village. To his left was Crag. No one wished Newton and his family a bad turn more than Crag. Their feeling toward him was no different. The giant was not one to open his ears once they took in what it pleased him to believe. "That one is led too much by a hunger in his belly," his mother had said of him. "A hunger for others to do for Crag without thought or question." His father spat back, "Yes, he is a troll whispering under the bridge, telling giants he will bear their weight when it is the bridge that carries them. He will not know of happiness until he leads the Elder Council. When that happens, the time of peace among giants will end." His parents had spoken out strongly against Crag's appointment to the Council, but, respected as they were, Crag was selected by the thinnest of margins. He could be slippery with his words. It was a gift that bore him beyond his hollow wisdom. His parents knew they had made a powerful enemy, but neither seemed concerned. They had friends of their own. And in the end, it was not Crag who betrayed them.

Thoughts of his parents pained Newton, even in his slumber-journeys. *Why does everything bring this giant back to what he did to them?*

To Gabroc's right was Pegma, the ancient giant and once High Elder. At 694 years, she was not the oldest in the land, but her boots had walked more than most. She was of a good wisdom of things, but more of things past than of the day. A Puncher followed close behind Newton, prodding him forward.

Back in the cave, Newton's fists clenched in his sleep. His breathing quickened.

The Punchers towered over the other giants. Knotty gray barklike skin covered deeply sinewed bodies, giving them the appearance of weathered trees. They were of a race of giants—the Apooncha—who dwelled far beyond the Oaken Hills. They'd never been known to speak, and Newton had heard that unlike giants of his kind, they did not turn to stone when frightened. Years ago, his friend Pryat told him that he once heard the Apooncha faint when taken by fear. However, he had added, no one he knew had ever seen one so taken.

Again, as many times before, Newton's slumber-journey continued his ascent up Makers' Ear, a tall hill at the edge of the city. Scattered below were the charred remains of homes, destroyed by the skyfire. *The problem is real*, thought Newton. *Their answer is not. I did not make this happen!* They reached the top by early afternoon. The Iron Thorn loomed before him. He had seen the pillar in the distance from his cell, rising like a spike driven into the crest of Makers' Ear. It was here an unfortunate giant would plead his innocence to the Makers, and here where the Makers may choose to open an ear to those pleas. The Makers spoke through spears of lightning. The firebolts from the clouds were drawn through the giant and into the iron spike. It promised that, whether the Makers were sympathetic or not, there was little chance of surviving such an exchange. Giants do not burn, but lightning is a different kind of fire. It cooks a body from the inside out. A dozen or so strikes is enough to pull a life from the strongest among them.

The tiny platform at the top disappeared in a swirling mass of black clouds, sporadically illuminated by the flashes of lightning.

"They gather," said Gabroc.

A Puncher waited at the base and began turning a large crank. The Thorn squealed, grinding against the sides of its sleeve as it sank into the ground.

"Step on, and do not turn to stone when They speak!" said Pegma. "It will be worse for you if you do. It brings a shame to all giants."

"And," added Gabroc, "you would shatter."

"He will turn," said Crag. "He is a coward."

"Would you be of a wish to go in my place?" asked Newton. "You could ask the Makers yourself if this giant's looking up at the stars brought the skyfire. They will answer *you*, of the Elder Council, if *you* do not turn."

"Nephrite has sent *you*, Broont."

"I am Newton, not Broont. If a giant can choose his name, why do you not honor mine?"

"It is not a giant's name," said Crag. "The tongue stumbles to speak it."

"Enough," said Pegma. "This giantess wishes this to end what you have begun, but she takes no joy in it. We do not question the Mother Shepherd of Holygiants. Nephrite speaks for the Makers, and it is she who sends you to them. I will call you Newton, if it will help you face them as the giant you believe you are."

Newton stepped onto the platform and tried to hold steady as it was cranked up into the air.

Back in the cave by the Fire Sea, the giant clutched at the air, his sleeping mind looking to escape what was about to happen. But escape never comes. His slumber-journeys always keep to the same path, the path he traveled back across the seas.

He was in the clouds. The smell of oily metal settled heavily in his lungs. He could taste it, like bitter rust on a cobbler's boot nail. Did it come from the clouds or the Iron Thorn itself? Arcs of lightning buzzed around him, lifting the hairs on the back of his neck. There was a break in the clouds, and he looked down. His escorts were walking away, down the hill, closer to safety. The Puncher at the base, impervious to anything anyone knew of, remained to prevent any giant from helping him. *But who would help this giant?* wondered Newton.

A lighting bolt struck him. It entered the top of his head, tore through his body and left through the soles of his feet, pinning him to the iron. When he could move again, he looked himself over, fully expecting to see strips of flesh and muscle hanging from his bones. From the outside, he appeared okay. He waited for another strike. The waiting brought fear, and he began to turn to stone.

"NO!" he shouted. He arched his back and strained to look up to the clouds. "What have you to say to this giant? Here is Newton! He does not fear you! You fear HIM! You fear what he sees!"

Zzzz-crrrackle . . . CRAACK! A screaming tor-hawk streaked through him, clawing at his insides, mad to escape anywhere it could find a way out. He was brought to his knees. There was no tor-hawk, Newton knew. But it was an image his body chose to understand the pain. He smelled fire. It was him. Black smoke billowed from his nostrils. His skin was hardening. Newton was beginning to turn again.

He sang. Somehow, it pushed away the fear.

"A giant's bones," he boomed, "are made of stone. A giant's roar brings the war . . ." He was struck again. Newton lost his footing and nearly fell from the platform. Had he done so, he would have likely turned to stone and survived the fall, but he knew the Puncher would send him back up before he turned back. He remembered what Gabroc had said would happen when the Makers spoke to a giant in that state. *This giant would be just more pebbles on the hill*, he thought. Newton grabbed on to the edge, but then rolled onto his back, to face the Makers. He continued to sing.

"When a giant's heart is torn apart. A giant's brave, to the . . ." The lightning continued to strike. Again and again. Over and over. The sound exploded in his ears. Through the cracking whips of searing light, he thought he heard his name called. *The Makers do speak?* Another spear of white-hot light crashed through his chest. It came out his back, arced down, and grabbed on to the Thorn. It held him in place as it rattled his body in agonizing spasms. And then struck again.

"Newton!" called a voice from what sounded like many lands away. The giant rolled onto his belly and looked over the edge. Through his nearly baked eyes, he could not see who it was, but he knew. Only one giant called him by his chosen name.

"Pryat?" he said to himself.

"Hold on. I am getting you down."

Well, fo fum, thought the giant.

SIX

Soup Pots and Dragons

Newton awoke, his face awash in sunlight that filtered into the cave. He had slept through the night. If his slumber-journeys took him elsewhere after his rescue, he did not remember. *And that is not always a bad thing.* Yet it was good to see Pryat again. Newton recalled how his friend had knocked down the Puncher at the base of the Thorn.

"How did you . . . ?"

Pryat pointed to a boulder a short distance away. It was nearly as big as he was. "I threw that at him. He fell. It is how I like Punchers—felled."

Newton crawled out of the cave. He stood and stretched. His hand was itchy. The giant brought it to his face and saw that his pinkie had turned to stone. It was turning back, slowly. *Odd,* he thought. The Makers' Voice inside him was now just a whisper. *Maybe the pain was left in the Newton that wakes when* this *Newton sleeps.* He felt bad for that other Newton. Did that Newton feel bad for him? What was he to do now? He could go back to the village, but maybe not just yet. He never found comfort in large gatherings, especially ones where so great a number of eyes were drawn to him. And the mans had so many questions. He wasn't sure which ones he should answer, although his tongue held little back. *If they want to know a thing, why should they not? We should all know all things. Maybe here that is not so bad.*

He shook his hand, trying to wake his pinkie. It was nearly back to normal. He gave it a wiggle. *"Humph . . ."*

The giant looked back up the shore, toward the woods that led to the village. He hoped to see Jat. *Maybe he is not coming.* The waves of flames rolled in the distance. He searched the horizon for the column of water, the great spinning *stalk of vines*, that had brought him here. Could it bring him back? It was of no matter. He couldn't find it, and if he could, he would not go back.

He thought again about the village circle. *Did I say a thing I should not have said?* He was used to asking himself this question. He thought he should probably ask it more. But what could they do to him? They were of such a small size. *Fum, a scree-mouse can bite. And what is a bite of a mouse but a nibble?* But could mans hurt him in a way he did not know? *Jat would not hurt this giant.* But not all mans were Jats. Some were Willowhocks. Some were Stoggins.

Newton would wait a while for Jat to come. And if he did not, *foomph*, he would see . . .

The giant sifted through the stones at the base of the cliff, looking for different colors to work with. He would use them to tell more of his story—even some of the parts he wished to forget. He was a giant who had done what giants did not do. He survived the Iron Thorn. He traveled across the Great Sea on a jumble of cobbletrees. Along the way he battled a sea serpent, and ate it, and discovered many strange new creatures. He walked beneath an ocean of fire. Maybe someday another giant would come this way and see what he had done. The thought pleased him. Sharing things that made his heart pound fast made it pound faster yet.

The giant drew all these things that lived behind his eyes. He remembered each one and could see them inside his head. At first, he used just lines: curves and arcs, circles and squares. They were like the markings in his silent speakers, but different— more like real things that he could touch. They looked like real things, at least. And he *could* touch them. The markings he had studied in his silent speakers back home made the words that *talked* about real things. Talked about them in his head. They were not as the things themselves. *These are more close*, he thought.

He accidentally smudged the lines that made his sister, Ooda. It added a shadow to her shape. She looked even more like Ooda. Ooda who hated him. Ooda who burned the barn where he hid his silent speakers and farlooker. Ooda who smashed all his waterstones. Ooda who pulled his ears. *Ooda whose parents I turned to Everstone. Of course she hates this giant for what he did.* He could not draw his parents. The sickness he felt in losing them was worse than that of the Makers' Voice in his belly.

He ground some of the stones to dust and used the palms of his hands to rub color and shading inside the lines. His story, his *life* came to live on the cliff wall.

Jat appeared at Newton's cave just after sunset. The Fire Sea's light flickered on the cliff wall, causing the images to shimmer and dance in place. Newton was busy rubbing dusty green scales on a great serpent that rose from the blue sea. He had given it four heads, even though the one he'd fought had only one. The extra heads made it look as if it were wiggling back and forth.

"Do you see this?" Newton asked excitedly. "They come alive! They move! Is this some kind of magic of your land?"

"I don't believe in magic," said the boy. "But seeing this, I almost do. It's pretty amazing, Newton."

"You have not seen this before?"

"No. I think the fire from the sea is making it happen. Like how candles make things look . . . jumpy. Shadows and things."

"Magic," said the giant. "Magic from the Fire Sea Makers."

"No," said Jat. "I don't know, but . . . no. Not magic. Not everything we don't understand is magic."

Newton raised his eyebrows. "You are right, Jat. Yes, you are right. I have said this myself! Are all mans of a wisdom like yours?"

Jat shrugged. "No."

Just then, Newton got a closer look at the boy's face. "What happened to you?"

Jat looked away, as if ashamed. "Nothing," he said. "I banged into a tree going to the outhouse last night."

"Your one eye has a dark circle around it. And . . ." Newton looked more closely. "Your lip is fat."

"Walked into a tree, Newton."

"And your ear is poofy, and purple!"

"AHH! STOP! I WALKED INTO A TREE! IT HAPPENS! Your whole FACE is poofy! How about that!"

Newton didn't believe his story, but he could tell Jat was not going to tell him what had really happened. "Tree thrumped you good," he said.

"Do giants have magic in their world?" asked the boy, changing the subject.

"We do have magic in my land, but only the holygiants know it. They cannot do this, though," said Newton, staring in awe at the dancing figures. "It only happens in the dark, it seems. Yes, the Fire Sea awakens my . . ."

"Drawings," said Jat.

"Oh yes! My *drrawings*. I have *drrawn* them from inside me. Do I live in their slumber-journeys? Or do they live in mine?"

"You ask strange questions, Newton. What's that nail in the hill?"

"*Harumph* . . . that is where the Makers spoke to this giant. It is where they put their voice in here," he said, patting his chest. "It is their voice that brings the pain. But I am feeling a little better now. I have told you of Pryat," he added, pointing to a picture of his friend. "He knocked down this Puncher with a boulder and rescued me. Punchers do not get thrumped, but Pryat did not care and thrumped him anyway."

Jat walked along the cliff, studying Newton's work. "Oh, those things," he said, pointing up to a series of little rectangles. "You talked about them to the village. What did you call them?"

"Silent speakers," said the giant.

"Yup, those look like books," said the boy.

"*Boooks*..." said Newton. "It is a word this giant has not heard. These silent speakers are as blocks of wood with thin sheets of wood bark inside. The sheets are marked with scratches that I have learned are a way of making words—of sharing the thoughts of who put them there. When I look at them, I see pictures behind my eyes. I hear silent words in my ears."

"Yes, books, like I said. We have those here, too."

"Well, we do not have them in my land, Jat," said Newton. "It took this giant many years to understand them. They spoke of lands in the sky. The stars are as suns for them. I found a way to make a thing so I can see these suns more closer." Newton pulled something out of his pocket and held it up in front of the boy. It was clear as the sky, and worn smooth and round.

"Glass, I think," he said. "You made this?"

"Yes. I call them waterstones. *Glassss*? I like that word. It sounds like the thing that it is when it breaks. I made this, and others. Then I made them smooth and round with a fine stone. If you hold it over a thing, it makes it look more big." The giant turned to the wall and rubbed his hand along an image of a long tube mounted on a base. "This is a farlooker. I saw this in one of the sil... *boooks* I found. A waterstone—*glassss*, like this one, at each end, brings the stars close to a giant's eye." Newton sighed. *It also brings trouble to curious giants.*

"What are those things you drew above your farlooker?"

"Skyfire. The holygiants and Council say that my looking at the stars has angered the Makers who live there. The Makers, they *say*, have sent their dragon to punish us with their burning rocks. They say that it sent one to burn our village as a warning. And that more will drop from the sky because of me. I have seen their dragon through my farlooker. *Fum*, it is no dragon. They are stars in the shape of a dragon. Like this . . ." Newton fished a soft white stone from his pocket and drew some dots on the wall. "This is their dragon. I think it looks more like a soup pot."

"I think I know that soup pot, or dragon, up there," said the boy. "I see it all the time. I always thought it looked like a big spoon. There is one in the sky next to it that's like a smaller spoon. When it gets a little darker, I'll show you— should be soon."

"I know that other one! It is here? It is in your land, too?"

"It is, or I think it is," said Jat. "If what you drew is what you saw back home, how far did you really travel?"

"I do not know," said the giant. "I thought very far, but now I do not know."

"My life got a lot more interesting with you showing up, wherever you came from."

Newton laughed. "Is that of a good thing?"

"It is very much *of a good thing*!" said the boy.

"When Ooda destroyed my farlooker, this could no longer travel," he said, pointing to his head, "to the lands of the Makers in the sky. But maybe this giant can find a way from over here."

"What's a ooda?"

"*Fum* . . . my sister. She feared the things this giant saw. She believed, like all giants, looking up close at the stars angered the Makers—that this giant was spying. And that they sent the Makers' Dragon, the one on this wall—the *soup spoon*—to punish us with skyfire."

"What happened to it?"

"She burned it. And she burned my *boooks*. She burned the whole barn down."

"I have a sister, too. But she's okay. She's real young, though. More annoying than anything. Doesn't burn things, which is good . . ."

"Mine is meaner than a sack of mudbadgers. And she got more meaner. After—"

"Look!" said Jat. "It's dark enough to see now!" He pointed up to the sky.

Newton sat back to look at the star cluster. "That is it!" he said. "It is the same from my land!" A flash of light blazed into view and quickly fizzled out. "Skyfire! You have skyfire, too! We are of the same land. When we look up, we see the same sky." The giant looked down at the boy, his face in open wonderment. "Mans live in giants' land. And giants live in mans' land. This giant is still . . . home."

"Wow," said Jat. He traced an arc in the air with his finger. Newton noticed his bruised knuckles but said nothing.

Then the giant gasped. "A thought this giant does not like just fell into this head. Did I bring the skyfire here? Were the holygiants of a truth in their claim?"

"Nah. It's been doing this since before you got here. Shooting stars, some people call them. I guess that's the thing you were calling skyfire. I like your name better. I once heard

Flora say that they are sometimes up there for a long time—for weeks—and that they're not real stars because they'd crush us if they were. I look at the stars a lot, too. There's really not much else to look at at night."

"But are you not of a fear of the fires your *stars that shoot* can bring?"

"They don't fall on us," said the boy. "Well, some might, but I've never seen it happen."

"*Hrmmph*," said Newton. "They have to fall to the land somewhere. Can the ones we see here fall beyond the Fire Sea, where the giants live?"

"Maybe. I don't know. It sounds like one of them did."

Newton was silent.

"You know," said the boy, "if one does land on us, then maybe it *is* your fault. But if one doesn't, then you know for sure it is not."

"I do not know if that thought pleases me," said the giant.

"I was only joking, Newton," said Jat. "Nothing from up there is coming down here. I wouldn't be sitting right next to you if I thought there was even a chance of it."

"This giant is grateful for that trust. And Flora is right. Those are not stars. They are burning rocks," said Newton.

"Rocks can't burn," said the boy. A streak passed overhead.

"Maybe the rocks do not know this, and burn just the same," said the giant. Then he pointed to the Fire Sea. "Seas do not burn, but look. They do."

"Maybeee . . . But that's just a name we gave it—*sea*. It's not a sea of *water*."

"Haroomph . . ."

"Anyway, I use the stars that *don't* fall to help find my way when I fish in the harvest season. And they tell me when winter is coming."

"You can become a fish?"

"No! Fish! *Catch* fish! We catch them and eat them."

"You *fish* on the Fire Sea . . . of *not water*. Do you catch fire fish?"

Jat smiled, or tried to through his swollen lip. "No. There are other oceans—real ones with salt water. They surround the Fire Sea but never cross it. I make the trip when the firetide coals get washed over with sand, always every year, always harvest season. Takes too long to dig them out between waves. I'll take you with me . . . Oh, I don't think you'd fit in my boat. It's not much bigger than I am."

"That is okay. I do not miss the water oceans. The Makers talk to you? Tell you where to go?" asked Newton.

"What are they—the Makers?"

"The Makers made giants and their land. They live above us, but too far to see. Some live beneath our boots, too, we are told."

"I don't know about them. But no, no one really talks. I just find my way by looking at where they are. The moon, too. It tells me things about weather, sometimes. But sometimes it's just a big round moon."

"And sometimes it is not," said Newton. "Sometimes it's just a chip of the moon, or no moon at all." The giant thought a moment. "They speak to you like my silent speakers."

"Yeah, like books, I guess, but you don't have to read

them. Well, you sorta do, but it's different," said Jat. "I still don't know how to read those—books. A little, maybe, some words, but not that much. My dad showed me some, but . . ."

"But?"

"Like you said before, 'It is a story that carries pain.'"

"The story of your father?"

"Yes," said the boy.

Newton heaved a great sigh. "We are filled with stories of pain, giants and mans both."

"It seems."

"Sometimes the pain eases with the telling."

"You tell me about yours, then," said Jat.

Newton huffed a sad laugh. "You hand me back my own words. But no, I will not speak of my mother or father. You cannot ask me about them, ever. It is a hurt in wait, hungry to feed."

"Okay."

They sat in silence, each lost in their thoughts. Then Newton turned to the boy.

"Jat?"

"What?"

"Is my face really poofy?"

"Yeah, but I think it's supposed to be."

SEVEN

Mans-Eating Giant

"When you're done yanking out those trees on the back edge, you can take a goat break," said Maynard Hinson. *A few goats would be nice*, thought Newton. It would top off nicely the flock of geese he'd eaten earlier from the lake. Geese were plentiful. He'd clear out a flock and a new one would settle in overnight. Pulling trees was hard work, even for a fifty-foot-tall, 3,600-pound giant. *But a word given is a word kept.* Hinson needed the space cleared to expand his farm, and he was getting too old to do it himself. Newton was happy he was able to help. Hinson seemed like a nice enough mans, although a little grumpful at times. The giant had added a plot of cabbages to his future menu by offering to dig the planting furrows for them. By dig, he meant drag his fingers through the dirt.

"About them goats," continued the old man. "You given any thought to cooking 'em first?"

"I still do not see why," said Newton. "It makes them taste like dry wood."

"Suit yourself. It's just some here get a little sick watchin' you eat."

"I know your ways are different, but there is no other way to put food in me."

"Well, them trees ain't gonna yank themselves out," said Hinson.

"I did not think they . . . oh, I understand. Go pull trees."

Over the next few months, the townspeople kept Newton busy. He had to admit, he enjoyed being his size—big. Back home, or what he used to think of as home, he was thought to be *not small* . . . but also not big. Here, he stood out, and aside from one accidental barn crushing—fortunately, it was empty at the time—he stood out in a good way.

He would be happier still if the Makers' Voice were gone from him. His insides still burned, growing steadily worse as the weeks went on. He knew he was damaged somehow but didn't know how to fix it. He had long since learned to make the pain flow from his body out into the air. It allowed him to live with it, but it was tiring. Occasionally, a finger, or toe, or an ear would harden, almost to stone. He wondered if this was because of what had been done to him. Or if it was something different. And would it get worse?

As he was heading home, he saw Jat. The boy was running down the street.

"Jat, wait!" called the giant.

Jat looked up at him as he ran. His nose was bleeding and

the sleeve was torn off his shirt. He looked away and continued running.

"Jat! Stop! What happened?" Then Newton saw three boys at the corner. They were doubled over laughing and patting one another on the back. "What happened to Jat? Did you do that to him? Are you the ones who have been hurting him?"

The three shrank back. Then Durd seemed to have gathered his courage and stepped forward. He was a sturdy boy, with close-cropped blond hair and small, squinting eyes. "My ma said you can't eat us. She said there is a witch's curse on you or something."

"I do not need a curse to not eat mans. Why do you keep hurting my friend?"

"He has a big mouth. He's dirty. And he smells like a stinkin' wet fireplace . . ."

"And he thinks he's better'n us," added Sack. Sack was Durd's younger brother, but he was a full head taller and half a body wider. "Like he doesn't know who we are."

"And what Bonnie did," said Mason Twirp.

"Shut up," said Durd, shoving his friend.

"No, he does not think that," said Newton. "He does not think he is better than any of you. This giant knows this. And he smells of the Fire Sea because he works hard there. Or he did. He is done with that now. And it was not a bad smell. He was of a smell of an honest boy who does what he must." Newton bent over and sniffed Durd. "*You* smell like the sour water dripping from under your arms. Should this giant *thrump* you?" He sniffed Sack. "So do you. Does this mean you should be thrumped?" Then he sniffed Mason Twirp, whose knees were shaking. "You do, too, and also of the water that is soaking your pants. Should this giant thrump you, too?"

"You can't!" said Sack. "Ma said . . ."

"If you ever hurt my friend Jat again, this giant will break the witch's curse and . . . *hrmph* . . . just . . ." It occurred to Newton just then that threatening to harm someone did not come easily to his tongue. It was something he'd never done. He scooped them up in his hands and held them to his face so they could see he was not light of jest.

Newton roared, "JUST . . . LEAVE HIM BE!"

He plopped the quivering boys back down and stomped away to Jat's house. *He will be happy this is over,* thought Newton. He wondered if he should tell him what he did, or if he should let him think they just grew tired of bothering him. *Jat did not want me to know what was happening. If I tell him what I did, he will know I was of that knowledge.*

By the time he arrived, Jat had cleaned himself up and changed his shirt. He acted as if nothing had happened. Newton would do the same.

The boy lived with his mother and young sister along the outer edge of the village bordering the Fire Sea. Jat had told the giant of how his father had died, just before his sister was born, while collecting coal in the tide. Jat had been forced to watch helplessly as the curling flames dragged his father to the sea. Now it was up to him to fend for himself and his family. Life had been hard for them. Their small piece of land was dry and sandy, ill-suited for growing food, so they took advantage of the one available resource nearby, as had generations of their family before them. Coal from the firetide burned longer and hotter than regular coal. And it was virtually smokeless. As valuable a fuel as it was, most regarded the risk in collecting it too great. It was also dirty and tiring work. A coal sprinter wore his trade on his skin and clothes. The dull gray coal dust clung to Jat's face. Streams of his sweat would leave behind long, pale streaks in the soot. It was unavoidable, and while it could be washed off, it took hours of scrubbing his skin raw. By the time he'd finished collecting the day's haul, he often chose sleep over the cleaning ritual he'd just have to endure all over again the next day. Jat had tried wrapping a cloth around his face, but to read the shifting tides he needed to feel the wind on the only part of his skin not covered. He cleaned up as best he could whenever he needed to head into town, but with only his reflection in a bucket of water to go by, it was hard to hide the stain of his trade.

But now it seemed their times of hardship were behind them. In just a few days, Newton had collected with his bare hands what would have taken Jat years of racing the firetide. The coal mound piled on their little patch of land dwarfed their cottage. It needed no shelter to keep it dry because rain simply rolled off its hard outer surface. The boy would never again have to risk the fate that had taken his father. He could walk proudly among the other boys and girls, his sparkling face free of the streaky dust that had branded him. And the townspeople would ride out the brutal winters in toasty homes heated with firetide coal.

But still he is beaten by slow-witted trolls. Maybe no more.

Abeleena sat in Newton's hand as he lifted her above the treetops.

"And down flies the little bird," he said, dropping his hand to the ground. The little girl squealed in delight.

"I hate watching you do that," said her mother.

"He won't drop her," said Jat.

"Just the same . . ."

"It is my regret, Fira. I will stop if it is your wish," said the giant. He tipped his hand and Abeleena tumbled gently to the ground, giggling.

"It's okay, Newton. Maybe I'm just jealous."

"Would you like to play diving tor-hawk?"

"No, thank you," said Jat's mother.

"Come on, Mother. You know you really want to."

Fira laughed. "Nope."

"Diving tor-hawk . . . Did your father play that with you?" asked Jat.

Newton's face turned blue with shame. He looked away from the boy. "We do not speak of my father."

"Your mother, then?" asked the boy.

Newton turned back to him, his face now flashing anger. Jat stepped back. The giant roared, "Do not speak of my family! I have told you this! I HAVE TOLD YOU THIS, JAT!"

Newton immediately regretted losing his temper. *When you hide a truth from a friend, guilt escapes on the back of anger . . .*

Abeleena screamed in terror and ran to her mother's arms. Fira's eyes grew wide as she cradled her daughter. Newton smelled the sour odor of man-fear and his features immediately softened.

"It is my great regret!" he said. "Little, little Abeleena, do not cry. This big oaf beast would never, never hurt you." The girl continued to wail.

"I'll bring her inside," said Fira. "You two go for a walk somewhere. Anywhere that's not here."

"But I . . ."

"It will be okay, Newton, but go. And don't you ever yell at my boy like that again."

"Never!" said Newton. "Never again! It is a promise!"

"Come on," said Jat. "Let's go to your place."

The two hiked to the cave where Newton was making his home. He had built himself a roof over the opening and was in the process of putting up walls on the sides. Giants don't particularly enjoy getting wet, so it was a comfort to have some shelter from the rains as he sat and gazed at the Fire Sea. He had come to enjoy the *sound* of rain, though, which surprised him. He found soothing the hissing of raindrops as they sizzled in the distant flames. It gave off the wistful mineral-rich aroma of drying lava.

The roof also kept his books dry. He enjoyed the collection of silent speakers, no, *boooks* the peoples had given him. Jat often joined him. He didn't know how to read very well, but he liked looking at the pictures in the ones that had them. The books were tiny in the giant's fingers, the words smaller yet, but he was fortunate to have the waterstone *glassss* he kept tucked into his shirt pocket. It helped make the tiny letters slightly less so.

Newton and Jat found themselves wandering along the cliff wall by Newton's home. They had no other plans for the rest of the day. Newton still felt bad about making the boy's sister cry earlier. And for yelling at his friend.

"You've been working on your wall story," said Jat. "Hey, is that me?" The giant had been experimenting with different rocks and plants with which to draw on the cliff.

"That is you. That is your mother. That is Abeleena . . . poor little Abeleena."

"She cries about everything," said Jat. "Don't worry about it. Your pictures are getting better. They look just like the real things, almost."

"Yes, they do," said Newton. "They are as my children. They were not here before I made them. Giants do not do this, Jat. No giant does this."

"I know. You've said that."

"I do not know why. It is easy, and it brings this giant joy."

"You are one special giant, I guess. If you weren't, you wouldn't be here."

"No, Newton is just Newton."

"And Jat is just Jat."

"Yes, Jat is just Jat," said the giant. He was silent a moment. "What will Jat do now? Now that he does not have to scoop coal."

"I've been thinking about that a lot," said the boy. "I think I want to be like you."

Newton laughed. "You want to be big? You want to be loud? You want to frighten little mans-girls?"

"No," he said. "Though I wouldn't mind being your size. I think I want to see what else is out in the land. If there really are giants, and I think it's safe to say there are, what else could there be? There have to be places like . . . like your lands in the stars, or your stalk of vines, places where there are new things to see—that I don't even know I'm missing."

Newton reached down and placed a gentle finger on Jat's head, careful not to push him over.

"*Haroomph* . . . Your boots walk outside of your head. You are like me already."

"But then I think about my mother. She lost Father, and now she would lose me."

"Yes, she would be sad," said Newton. "But she once left her mother. And her mother once left her mother. Sons leave mothers. If they did not, their homes would be crowded villages of mothers and sons and *their* sons and mothers."

"We do have enough coal, so she wouldn't need me. At least for a few years. She won't have to worry about food or paying land fees to Lord Ellery, thanks to you."

"I think you would miss her, too. I will tell you about my mother and my father someday, Jat. Just not now."

"Okay. But trust me. There is NO way I will be the one to bring it up—again."

"This giant has to ask . . . why *did* you up-bring it? You know it is not a thing you should do."

"I don't know, Newton. I don't know why I do that. Mother says I . . . seem to need to prove that someone likes me even when they're mad at me. To test them? I don't know if that's what I'm doing. It's not on purpose. She usually says that when I make her mad. Maybe she's right. It's stupid. I need to stop doing that."

"Do they still like you when you have made them mad? Is that a mans thing?"

"Do you see me surrounded by adoring friends?"

"This giant is your friend still."

"My only one. But thanks." Jat looked out at the Fire Sea. "And yeah, I guess I'd miss my mother. But I would visit her when I could. And I'd have great stories to tell her."

Newton winced.

"The pain?" asked Jat. The giant nodded but waved it off.

"You are still young," he said. "You have hundreds of years for your boots to walk the lands."

"Hundreds of years? How long do you think we live? How old are you?"

Newton thought a moment. "I think I am of one hundred and forty-two years. Maybe one hundred and forty-three. Still young, like you."

"Hog's lard! One hundred and forty-three? Years? No one here even comes close. Mother said Flora is about eighty-something, and *that* is old. She's the oldest person I know."

"Oh, *fo fi*," said Newton. "I am still young. You are still young." Then he thought a moment and frowned. "But eighty-something is old for mans? I will still be a young giant of two hundred and you will be Old Jat. Your boots are almost worn to the sole! Maybe you should do what you wish, and do it soon. Do it now! Eighty years is just a snap of a finger. A sniff of a nose!"

"I will," said Jat. "Someday soon."

The giant's massive face scrunched in concern. "Someday soon is almost now. You will be *dead* soon, dead in a . . . clap of my hands. I miss you now, Old Jat, and you are still Young Jat."

"I AM still here. YOUNG Jat. Don't worry."

"But you won't be. You will be gone . . . very soon! Burn the Makers! My old friend dies as we sit."

"Okay, Newton. GAH! That's enough!"

The giant lifted his head. "Do you smell that?"

"No, what?"

"Horse-ox."

"There you are!" shouted a voice.

"Constable Stoggin!" said Jat.

The constable rode his horse across the sand, his face flushed with anger. Bonnie and Thumbridge followed. They climbed down off their horses and approached the giant and the boy.

"What's wrong?" asked Jat.

"You know what is wrong, boy," the constable said.

"No, I don't," said Jat.

"Then yer giant does."

"This giant does not, either. Is there trouble?"

"Yes," said Thumbridge, pushing forward. "YOU! You're the trouble. You threatened to eat three boys!"

"This giant did no such thing!"

"According to the Fengiss boys, you told them you were tired of eating geese and cows and it was time to try something new. Four people in the village saw you pick them up and hold them to your mouth!"

"They are lying!" said Jat. "Newton would never lay a hand on anyone!"

"Durd said he pried your fingers open and escaped."

"I had a little problem with that part of their story," muttered Bonnie.

"No," said Newton. "They are not lying. But also, they are not speaking in truth." He told them what had happened. Jat listened in silence. By the time Newton was finished, the boy was staring angrily at the sand at his feet.

"So you did not threaten to eat them, but you threatened to hurt them?" asked Stoggin.

"Good!" said Bonnie. "They're white-livered mudclods!"

"NOT good!" snapped the constable. He looked up at

Newton. "You can't go threatening white-livered mudclods. That's *my* job!"

"This giant never told them he would hurt them," said Newton. "I told them to stop hurting my friend. I would tell them that again. I would tell *you* that if *you* were hurting my friend! We are free to tell others to stop doing things we want them to stop doing. We stand up for our friends!"

"And if they didn't?" asked Thumbridge. "Stop? If they didn't stop?"

Newton thought a moment. He honestly did not know what he would have done. "This giant can only say to you that he would not have harmed them. And even more, he would not have *eaten* them!"

Constable Stoggin glared at the giant. No one said anything. Jat continued to stare down at the sand. Bonnie crossed her arms impatiently.

"Well?" she asked.

"Don't rush me," said Stoggin. Then he added, "Okay. I'll believe you. But listen to me, and listen good, giant. You make people nervous—*some* people . . . Willowhock won't shut up about you. And you make *me* nervous, which is a big problem for you. But so far, up to today, you've caused me little trouble. You can't go pickin' people up and scarin' their pants wet. Especially when it comes to the two Fengiss snobbers. I don't need no trouble from their family. If you have a problem with someone, you tell me. Or my boy."

Bonnie cleared her throat loudly. Stoggin squinted at her and frowned. He looked back up at Newton. "Me, or the boy. Got it?"

Newton hung his head in shame. "I do," he said.

"Boy?" he said to Jat. "You gotta control your giant. Got it?"

Jat didn't look up but gave half a stiff nod.

"And listen," said the constable to Jat, a little less angrily. "I know these boys are trouble. It ain't just you. They're gonna get theirs one day, but"—he pointed up to the giant—"it can't be from one of these things."

"No," said Bonnie, rubbing her fist. "It will be from someone who'll give it to 'em worse."

Constable Stoggin rolled his eyes. They got on their horses and rode off. Thumbridge turned and waved a warning finger at the giant. Budge came riding down the beach. The constable shook his head in frustration and motioned for him to turn around and join them. Budge stole a quick nervous look at the giant and tried to keep up with the others.

Newton didn't know what to say to his friend. Jat still stared at the sand, as if trying to burn holes through it with his eyes.

"*Hrm* . . ." said the giant. "That worked out okay. Constable Stoggin is a fair mans if one were to judge such a thing . . ."

Jat stalked away.

"Jat? It is my great regret I did not tell you. I knew you did not want me to know . . ."

The boy kept walking.

EIGHT

Isaac Newton

A few days passed with no visit from his friend. Newton went to his house, but Fira didn't know where he was. She hadn't seen much of him and was growing worried.

"Would you tell him I came looking for him?" asked Newton.

"I think he's mad at you about something. What did you do? No, what did *he* do, is probably a better question. No, actually, it could be either one of you . . ."

"This giant talks too much, Fira. Maybe it would be best if this time I said nothing."

He is not treating his friend as he should, he thought, stomping back to his home. *I helped him, did I not? Is this another one of his tests of friendships? Maybe this giant should stay away from* him *for a time!*

The next day, Newton went into town to deliver some

stones for a new house foundation. In exchange he was to receive some fat ropes to hold up his boots. While the fire from the Fire Sea had no effect on the old ropes—a giant's clothes are as impervious to flame as a giant—the salt from his journey across the Great Sea had slowly eaten them away. Newton's floppy boots were causing him to lose his footing more often than the townspeople felt comfortable with. As angry as he was at Jat for the boy's anger at *him*, he was less angry today than the day before. He hoped he would find him. He wanted to know why what he'd done was so bad. He saw Mason Twirp crossing the road. *He might know where Jat is.* The giant started to head toward him but then stopped. *It would be best to stay away from him. Too many eyes watching my every breath. Too many mouths to say they saw what did not happen.* Newton had grown used to being watched. He knew his size still made mans curious about him.

"Hey, giant!"

Newton turned toward the voice. "Hello, Flora," he said.

"I've been hoping to run into you, not that you're too hard to find. But I don't get into the village that much anymore. Do you have a moment?"

"Do you know where Jat is?" asked the giant.

"No, is he missing?"

"Yes, but of his own choice, this giant believes."

"He'll turn up," said the old woman. "No, I've been think-ing a lot about you. Can we speak?"

Newton frowned and sat down on the pile of boulders he dropped on the ground. "Can we speak?" was never followed by words he wished to hear.

"I would like to talk to you more about something you

said a while back. About how you taught yourself how to read."

"Oh!" said Newton, relieved. "That is something that would please this giant to speak about!"

"Believe it or not," said Flora, "I was a teacher in my younger days. Taught half the people here when they were kids, and then *their* kids. Don't like the word 'was,' though. We never stop thinking of ourselves as teachers. It's something in us. Something we *do*. I would love to know how you taught yourself to read. And maybe in exchange, I can teach you a little. I remember you saying that there were 'big empty spaces' in your understanding. I could maybe help fill them."

"This giant would be happy for your help. No giant has read words in *boooks* because we have no *boooks* to hold words. No giant has ever thought to make them."

"You do have a history, though, yes? Stories about things that have happened to others before you? I assume you pass it down with stories told mouth to ear?"

"Yes. Mouth to ear, then ear to mouth. Then mouth to next ear. But when a mouth is gone, its stories are lost. In *boooks*, they can tell the stories long after that mouth goes silent. They speak to the eyes instead of the ears, but it goes to the same place."

"But how can anyone start from nothing—from no-such-thing-as-books—and go to reading books about things so few understand, even here, where we *have* books?"

"*Hrump*," said Newton. How could he explain what he had done? He never thought much about how he did things. He just did them. And then got his ears pulled for it. "This giant's understanding came slowly, seasons upon seasons. I looked and looked and looked at the markings—*letters*, you mans call them—on the bark . . . no, *pages*. The letters . . . held open my head, like a stick propping open an oaken door on a day of snapping winds."

"You do have a way with words, giant," said the old woman.

"Thank you. Ooda, my sister, is of a thought that I use too many. With my head open, the great ideas lifted by the snapping winds—from the *boooks*—fell inside." He held his hands up and wiggled his fingers, dropping them down to patter like raindrops on his head. "After a passing of some time, I could look at a page of letters and not always *understand* each mark, but *feel*, and sometimes . . ." He sniffed loudly. "Smell, the bigger thoughts of the giants, or mans, or who or what it was that scratched the letters on the pages. Even the empty spaces *around* the words helped this giant learn their meaning. They are as thoughtful *breaths*. And Flora." He bent low to bring his massive face to hers. "They filled Newton's own life with meaning." He sat back up. "But yes, there are many words I still cannot understand. This giant feels he is missing large mouthfuls of the stories his eyes swallow."

"You are something we don't see a lot of; something we need," said Flora, her throat choking up with emotion. "Come see me tonight. I can teach you how to better understand what you were reading. But maybe there are things we can teach each other. And bring young Jat. He's been putting off learning how to read long enough."

"He is angry at this giant. It would just be me alone."

"I thought you two were the closest of friends. I never see one without the other."

Newton's lips tightened. He didn't know what to say.

"Friends fight. That's okay, Newton. In the end, you sometimes become even closer friends. Come tonight. We'll share some words."

That evening, back at home, Newton stepped out his door to leave for Flora's. He lingered a bit longer, hoping to see Jat bouncing down the beach. His anger had faded, turning to concern. He did not care who was mad at who. *I do not like this*, he thought, and left his home.

Flora waited for him in her chair outside her front door.

"You're late. The light's almost gone," she said. Newton bent down closer to try and read the expression on her face. She wore her usual frown. *But it is not a real frown. It does not reach her eyes.* Her silvery hair was neat as always, every strand held in place by a tightly knotted red ribbon on the back of her head. He gave a light sniff and smiled. *She is happy I am here . . . but there is a sadness?*

"It is my regret," said Newton.

"Actually, your lessons can wait. I have something else you'll find interesting. Heh! I certainly do. This'll knock you down and shake you up." Flora sat back and closed her eyes. Her arms were crossed, hugging her body. Her frown softened. She opened her eyes and looked up at Newton. The old woman unfolded her arms and held out two books. Newton gasped! He had seen one of those books before, or one just like it. She handed it to him.

"It is . . . the silent sp—It's the *boook . . . by!*" Newton slapped his chest, his face awash in amazement. "It is where this giant's name comes from!"

Flora smiled and nodded. "I thought so. Newton didn't sound like a giant's name, not that I know what a giant's name sounds like. But surely not *Newton*. And when you mentioned coming across a crate of books, made of pumice—you said 'stone,' but it was pumice—things began to come together."

The giant stared at the tiny book in his fingers. He flipped through a few of the pages with his fingernail, as he had done so many times for so many years. The words that had taken him so far now brought him right back home. "New-ton," he said softly. "But how is this? My *boooks* were burned back home! How can this one be here?"

"There are copies," said Flora. "I'm guessing you read others by men who studied the sky. Galileo?"

"This giant thinks so, but was saying it wrong inside his head."

"I think I have a copy inside. Not mine, but . . . Copernicus?"

"YES! But I was hearing that one wrong, too."

"Might have that as well. Those are the only ones I can think of. I tried reading them, but they're not for me."

"There was one by *Hal-lee*. And one by *Cass-eeneee*. *Ty-ko*? Or *Ticho*? Their words were big on the silent speakers, and I believed them to be the names of the speakers who made them. But some words are made different in the different *boooks*. This giant wondered if they came from places where they spoke different words for the same things."

"They did. That's part of the reason I couldn't read them—can't read other languages. You could?"

"Yes. In a way. Thoughts are thoughts are thoughts, no matter the sound of the words they ride on. But you have the one that . . . this giant chose his name from."

"Mm-hmm, Isaac Newton. He lives, or lived, in a faraway land. He might still be around. I don't know. In a place called *Anglund*, I think. I found this in a crate of books my late husband, Theobold, left behind. This was a newer one of his, and his favorite. I think partly because it was in the language we speak. He had two of them. You had the other one. It had to be his, and then yours. When he could, he'd collect two of every book, one for reading and one for preserving—for future 'seekers of knowledge.' He said he couldn't always understand what he was reading, but he kept at it because he heard stories about the man who wrote it. This Newton used something that sounds like your farlooker to study the stars and other things in the sky. Called it a *teleoscope*, I think. Something like that. Theobold spent all this time staring at these pages, grousing about how his brain was too small to understand what it meant. He was not an educated man. I shouldn't say that. He was very educated, but everything he learned, he'd learned on his own." She paused, as if in thought. "Like you, Newton . . . It all seemed a great struggle to him. But, heh . . . struggle he did. He talked about how he needed a teleoscope of his own, but he never actually made one." She waved her hands in the air and looked up at the darkening sky. "He'd go out night after night staring at the . . . blasted stars. Out 'til morning, he was. Sometimes I'd find him sleeping in the grass, the fool soaked in dew."

"What happened to him?" asked Newton.

"Theobold left me, said he needed more of these books to make sense of the things. And that he couldn't find them by sitting here, waiting for them to show up. Said he'd be back, of course—with answers. *Promised* me. He *promised* me . . ." A momentary look of sadness crossed the old woman's face. *That was what I smelled earlier*, thought Newton. She shook it off. "But he said there can be no more important thing than understanding the world. It's why people are here and what people are meant to do. I don't agree with that. I think there is more to why we are here, but that doesn't matter, I guess . . . Anyway, he said it was like a big question we have to answer, one small clue at a time, and when that was done . . . Well, he didn't know. He didn't know if it *could* be done. Does anyone? He was the most frustrating of men sometimes." She laughed. "Yep. Somehow he found a place where the Fire Sea joined up with our ocean, a place where it was not fire but, he said, almost like scalding water. And red. He said the water would be hot, but the boat would not burn. He covered the bottom with sheets of lead. Then he made a tight crate out of stone—pumice, which floats—to collect the books and keep them safe should something happen to him."

"And that is what I found," said Newton.

"Yes," said Flora. "It seems he found quite a few *clues* to his *question* before . . ." She paused. "I'm guessing his boat sank. When you told me about your 'silent speakers' bundled in a stone crate, I knew where they came from, and . . . I learned the fate of my husband."

"It is my regret, Flora," said the giant.

"Mine too," said the old woman. "He chose the mysteries of life over his wife. But who wouldn't? Well, I wouldn't have chosen it . . . over my husband. But different people are different, aren't they."

"Yes, Flora. Different peoples are different. So are the same ones—different."

"Keeps life from getting too boring. Anyway, knowing what happened to him is better than not knowing, I suppose. And," she added with a smile, "he didn't come back, but look who came instead! His books found their way into the right hands. I don't think even *he* could have imagined how big those hands would be."

Newton handed the book back to Flora. The old woman pushed it away.

"No, I don't want it," she said. "It's yours."

"I . . . I cannot take this," he said.

"You will," said Flora. "I lost my husband to that book. You lost your land to its ideas. I don't want it. Do *you* really? Look where it's brought you. You can have the others like it, if you wish."

Newton smiled. "This giant is happy where it brought him because it brought him to you. Thank you, Flora. I will think of Theobold when I look to the stars. He will travel with me. And with him, his wife."

"And now you will show me how well you've learned to read. How one can learn with no knowledge of written words, or that words can even *be* written, is still beyond me. We'll save your book of stars for another time, though. Let's see how you do reading this to me." She handed him another book.

"What is this?" asked Newton.

"Theobold's journal. His first one. His newer one went with him. He used this to collect his thoughts on his search for answers to his questions, what he was trying to understand. I would like to *hear* his words again. And I think you might find interesting his journey to know this world, and beyond."

"What is a 'world'?" asked Newton.

"It is a place of many lands. It is where we live," said Flora.

The giant opened the journal and read to Theobold's wife.

Flora had fallen asleep by the time it became too dark to read. Newton stood up and slipped away, silent as a giant could. He made it back to his home and lingered in front of his wall drawings. The flickering light from the Fire Sea made his characters dance and twitch. The pain inside him returned, doubling him over. He fell in front of the drawing of himself with the cows in his belly. Newton grabbed his real belly. There were no ox cows in there now. Just the burning of the Makers' Voice.

The giant picked up a red stone and scribbled fire over the cows he had drawn. "Take the fire from me, Newton on the wall!" He dropped to the sand and rolled over to rest his back against the face of the cliff. It slowly subsided.

"A bad one?" asked a voice.

Newton looked down. "Yes, Jat. A bad one." A long silence followed. "This giant is not angry with you anymore."

"What? You were angry with ME? You have that completely backward!"

"Yes, I was, but am not now. I am happy you are here." The giant stared at the boy. The light of the Fire Sea bathed his face in orange, bringing an eerie pulsing glow to his newly acquired bruises and scrapes. Jat made no attempt to hide them this time.

"I thought I had stopped them from doing this," said Newton. "They still attack you?"

"No, I attacked them."

"All three?" Jat nodded. "Did it bring it to an end?"

"No. It probably made things worse. But, Newton, I did it myself. I had to!"

"No, Jat. You did not have to."

"But I did! First Bonnie makes me feel like a helpless child by coming to my rescue. Then you do it. Then Constable Stoggin makes me feel like a tiny flea IN FRONT OF BONNIE again! In front of you . . . Why doesn't anyone think I can take care of myself?"

"This giant has seen how that was not working. A friend does not let a friend face danger alone."

"No, but a friend trusts his friends. You need to trust that I am able to solve my own problems. If I need help, I'll ask for it, like I did with the firecoal. Trust me, even if it makes me look like a fool! You can't even understand that? How weak you made me look?"

Newton gave this some thought. Yes, he could under-stand it. *I do not agree with it, but I do understand how one could think it.* "I will trust you even if it makes you look like the biggest bloody-nosiest fool in the land," he said.

"Thank you."

"But this giant is afraid your face is not up to my trust. You are starting to look like me."

"Ugh . . . now you insult me?"

"Looking like me is of a bad thing?"

Jat looked up at the giant and winced. "Ugh!"

"But if you ever need me to talk to them again, just . . ."

"WHAT? What was I just saying?"

"My regret. My regret. No more angry words for the stinky, fighty mans-boys. You can be the bloody-nosiest fool if that is your wish. You can be the bloody-nosiest fool who gets thrumped into the *fo fum* dirt every day of your *fo fum* short life. It is just hard on this giant's heart."

"I know. But some things you can really mess up by helping in the wrong way."

"Just wanted to . . ." mumbled Newton. ". . . friends help when . . ."

"Okay, how about you EAT them for me? Like they said you were going to do. Will that make you happy? Bite them in two!"

"NO! THIS GIANT DOES NOT EAT MANS! EVERY-ONE SAYS HE DOES, BUT HE DOES NOT!" He huffed and looked insulted. Newton turned back to the boy. "And if I did, I would then have to eat Constable Stoggin, and then Thumbridge, and then Bonnie. And delicious Budge! It would never end!"

"Then forget it. Stay away from them like we agreed."

Newton squinted, studying the boy. "Oh, you were of jest."

"Did you say *delicious* Budge?"

"Hoomph!"

The two sat in silence. Finally Newton said, "Your mother is worried about you."

"I know. I wanted to wait until some of the swelling went down before I saw her. But I might as well go now."

"Will you come back tomorrow?"

"Yeah."

Jat stood up and walked away. Newton watched him disappear down the shore. *A friend can bring a worry and anger greater than one's enemies*, he thought. *But still, a friend is better.*

He reached into his pocket and pulled out the book Flora

had given him. Her husband's book. *My boook!* How could something that brought so much light to his heart pull such fear and darkness from the hearts of others?

Newton closed the silent speaker in his hand, so tiny within his fingers, but so large inside him. It was where his name came from. He always liked the way that word looked, and the way he thought it would sound: *New-ton. Isa-ac New-ton.* And here it was in this land. This *world*. This is where he belonged.

NINE

Glassss

It was the coldest winter anyone could remember. The season hit the people hard every year and was endured in near isolation within their dusky homes. The cold would creep in and just sit there, on top of them. The boarded windows did little to keep the wind's icy fingers from clawing inside. In the warmer seasons, thin animal hides stretched over the window openings kept out the rain and insects while letting in a little hazy light. Glass for windows was rare, mostly set aside for the homes of lords and others of a high status. A typical village home was a small cottage riddled with holes and cracks, capped with a leaky thatched roof. Smoke-belching fireplaces kept most warm, or at the very least *alive* through the winters. Keeping them burning was endless work, and few wandered far from shelter. Winter life typically consisted of huddling for warmth, day and night, around smoky fires that needed constant tending. Coughing was a sound of the season. The harshness of this period was what kept this village from becoming more than a small settlement. Over time, the world outside had forgotten them. It was on no map. It had no name, even to the people who lived there. It was just where they were.

Had it not been for the blessing of a steady supply of Fire Sea coal that winter, some would not have lived to see spring. A half bucket would burn for a full day. It glowed with a clean, orange heat that seeped into every corner of the room. A well-worn path ran through the chest-high snow from Jat's home to the village. People brought them food, tools, and other trinkets in exchange for their firecoal. Eban Wiggs offered his daughter in marriage for five bucketfuls.

"She is a good cook and has strong arms; she can lift a boar over her head," he boasted.

"If you have no coppers, you can take what coal you need," said Fira. "We'll let no one freeze on account of money. It is too recent in memory *we* were in need." Jat tried to hide behind his mother. Sabrina Wiggs was twenty winters older than him and had only three teeth in her mouth.

"Thank you," said her father. "You are very kind. Your son would make a fine son to me, though."

"I'm sure he would," said Fira. "But he makes a fine son to me, too."

Newton had finished his home earlier in the season. It was a massive structure that jutted out from the great ledge on the shores of the Fire Sea. Entire trees made up the walls and roof. He left several openings in the sides to allow in more light, and he built a ladder leading to a big hole up top. Upon the roof was a series of ladders and platforms that brought him above the cliff wall and allowed him to see the sky in all directions. His evenings were spent gazing at the stars on the uppermost platform. He knew that they would speak to him, as they spoke to Jat. They would tell him things he did not even know he did not know. Giants had existed for ages with only a rare few bothering to look up. Part of it lay in the physical difficulty in doing so. They simply weren't built for it. Newton wondered about this often. *Could it be that we grew this way because we never look up? Or were we like this to start, so keep our eyes to the ground?* Since his early days, Newton had worked on giving his eyes more to see. He would lift his chin and hold it in place for as long as he could, strengthening neck muscles little used in giants. Over time, he found he could see eight giants high over the horizon without bending his back. Others seeing this thought it a very odd sight. "Look, Broont, a fat worm squeezing from ground," Ooda had once laughed.

However such things came to be, and however it sat with certain giants, there was no discomfort in *lying down* and looking up, which is how Newton spent much of his time.

The cold didn't bother him. They had far worse winters than this back in his land, and even those were shrugged off by the giants. The worst thing about this weather was the boredom. Most people stayed indoors. The giant enjoyed being with the villagers, mostly. He did need his time away from them, being of a type who savored his time alone. But he was afraid of enjoying solitude too much, of becoming a giant who starves himself on an empty feast of thoughts and knowledge that came only from himself. While there was less for him to do, he still found ways to pay for the food he ate. *Give first; then take. Give-take. It* does *work,* he thought. *But take-give is a little more better. There is less waiting for what a giant wants.* The surrounding forests and lakes were rich in food. His balance with the people was good. In fact, if it weren't for him, all their homes and roads would be buried under the snow. After every storm, he'd head to town and tromp paths with his feet. He directed some of the trails to his home, where he would welcome a visit on a winter evening, but only a few hardy souls took him up on it. Part of it was the distance in the cold weather, but another part was likely the fact that, harmless as he proved to be, giants still made most people a little nervous.

One time, though, he had a visitor who made *him* a little nervous. It was a *womans*, he believed. She wore a long cloak with a deep hood. He could not see who she was. She stood atop the cliff, looking down at him a good distance from his home. When he called out to her, she disappeared. He never saw her again but thought about her now and then.

Surprisingly, unless one was practically on top of it, the Fire Sea was stingy with its heat. It held close to its surface what would have been a gift of warmth for shivering souls. Otherwise, the villagers might have been inclined to migrate to the coast when the weather grew cold. Jat, however, went there nearly every day. It was where his friend lived.

"Mr. Willowhock is making trouble again," he said.

"I accept that I cannot have a friend in everyone," said Newton. "I have asked him how I can make balance. He says, 'Just give me cows!' I told him I cannot. I told him it is my regret. I told him you cannot make what happens not happen after what happens happens. And I have been telling him this since the day I stepped onto this shore! How can he not be as weary of hearing it as this giant is of saying it?"

"Well, he's bothering Lord Ellery about it. He rode all the way up to Ellery Manor, in this snow. Jacob Boarhutch said that he has been trying to gather men to drive you away."

"The Boarhutch mans is this giant's friend!"

"I know. I'm just saying what he said. He actually told Mr. Willowhock to . . ." The boy looked behind him instinctively. "I can't say the words, but he told him to do it. He thinks that Lord Ellery might summon the king for a troop of soldiers. I don't think he will, though. I don't think Lord Ellery wants to remind the king we're even here. At least that's what my mother says. It's more bother for him. The constable and Stoggin's boys don't want to have anything to do with any of this, by the way. So that's good. I *told* you about Mr. Willowhock, Newton. He gets this way and never, ever lets things go. I heard he still says a nightly curse for the nurse who once pinched him when he was a baby."

"He cannot remember that," said Newton.

"Like I said. He . . . never . . . lets . . . things . . . go!"

"But a troop of soldiers because of some skinny ox cows? I have not been a . . . *thief* . . . since then. It has been give-take since then. This giant has been kind to the peoples since then. As they have been kind to him."

"He is not saying so much about what you did, though he never stops going on about it, but what you *could* do. He doesn't like that if you decide you want to . . . flatten our village or something, it would mostly be up to you. More than *mostly*, actually. Remember that 'potential' thing we talked about a long time ago, when we first met?"

"I do not."

"Um . . . 'porridge'?"

"Oh, yes . . . something that can happen even if it is not . . . I would like to flatten the Willowhock, but I do not. But I would like to."

"Me too," said the boy.

"I do not know about Lord Ellery," said the giant. "I once brought him two handfuls of wet brown dirt for his gardens. It was meant a greeting. He did not come out, but I saw him peeking from behind a door."

"You make him nervous, too, is my guess."

"Isn't he your leader?" asked the giant.

"He owns the land, but he really doesn't have too much to do with us. Lady Ellery is usually the one people get to talk to. I heard she's okay, but I don't know a lot about either one of them. That's probably good, I guess."

"And your king? He is of a larger size than Lord Ellery?"

"His actual size?" Jat shrugged. "I don't know. That's not how you pick a king here. But if you mean is he more important, I'm sure he is. But he's far away, so it really doesn't matter."

"We—giants, that is—don't have kings."

"Who's in charge, then?"

"The Elder Council and holygiants. They are not as friends, but they are of a mind to work together. It is the only way to keep peace in our land. We like to fight, we giants do. If no one stopped us, there would be no giants. We would thrump one another into the ground until the ground and giants were no more. We were almost *no more* many times. Then we found a way, and it has been that way beyond what our eldest can remember."

"You don't seem like you like to fight," said Jat. "In fact, I bet I could beat you up. I could *thrump* you into the ground!"

Newton laughed. "Brave and mighty Jat finally defeats the water-pants Twirp mans-boy, and now he can defeat a great and powerful giant?"

"You should have seen him run home crying. You're next!"

Newton laughed again. "No, this giant does not like to fight. Please don't thrump him! As a giantling, maybe, with friends, surely, fighting was a thing of joy. But that went away. For this giant, at the least. The holygiants use their magic to speak to the Makers. The Makers tell them They do not wish for us to thrump one another into the ground. I do not think They want little firecoal boys to thrump giants, either."

"Oh well," said Jat.

"Oh well," said Newton. "The holygiants tell the Elder Council to make a way for us to live together. Sometimes that way to live together is better for the holygiants and Elder Council than for a giant like Newton."

"I think it's like that with kings and lords, too. So what are we going to do about Mr. Willowhock?"

"You will defeat him in battle for me, yes? Send him home crying to his mother?"

"Oh, I don't think he ever *had* a mother," said the boy. "But no, really!"

"This giant would rather think about mans who like him than mans who do not."

"Yes, people *like* you, Newton. But it might come down to which is more important, liking Newton or being made to fear him. Mr. Willowhock will keep bothering. He's plain stubborn, and Lord Ellery just wants problems to go away. He'll do what is easiest for him. Mr. Willowhock might convince him you are dangerous and that it would be easier in the long run for you to move on."

"What can they do to me? I do not boast, but I do not think peoples can hurt me much," said Newton. "Except you, Jat, of course," he added with a smile, and then with his finger, gently knocked the boy off his feet.

"Probably not," said Jat, standing back up. "But this can be serious. You found a way to fit in here, and I know you like it. It's home. If you were forced to fight us . . . them, not me of course, or Mother, or a lot of people, *most* people . . . would you? You know you'd win easily, but . . ."

Newton's shoulders slumped in defeat. "I would not. I would leave. I see what you say. I wish ox cows could be planted like beans in a field. I would grow them and make the balance." Then he lifted his hands in the air. "This all happened in a time far behind us. I cannot think about it anymore. *Fo fum*, bony old Willowhock. I have something to show you." The giant reached into his pocket and pulled out his waterstone. "I am of a thought to make more of these. I can make them for the village, but big and flat. They can fill your empty wind-eyes. You can see through them and keep out the cold and rain. You call them *windows*, yes? Oh, and I will also make a new . . . teleoscope to sit atop my roof."

"Can I help?" asked Jat.

"I was of great hope my friend Jat would help! With the firetide coals we can make a strong heat. We can make a lot of . . . what do you call waterstone?"

"Glass."

"Yes, *glassss*. *Glassss* windows for all my friends. But none for *fo fum* Willowhock."

"You can make him a glass cow."

"A *glasss* Willowhock with *glasss* ox cow uddlers," said Newton.

"A glass cow with Mr. Willowhock's head—his glass lips saying moo!"

Newton laughed. "I am of a thought that *glasss* can be made into many shapes, but windows and teleoscope first."

"What do you need to make it?" asked the boy.

Newton smiled. "Everything we need is here beneath our boots."

Jat looked down. "There is sand beneath my boots."

"Yes, there is."

"You can't see through sand."

"You can if you melt it," said the giant.

"You can't melt sand! It's . . . sand! It's small rocks!"

"We spoke of this already, Jat. Remember? Skyfire, or shooting stars? This giant is of a thought that anything can be melted if you make it hot enough. A time ago, I watched lightning melt the ground. It struck the sand at the edge of the Great Sea. Where it struck, I found little clear rocks. Lightning turned the sand into this waterstone. I thought, '*Newton, if you can make fire hot as lightning, you can melt sand, too.*'"

"Newton—spinning my head round in circles again . . ."

Newton laughed. "HA! You remind me of someone," he said.

"Someone dizzy?" asked Jat.

"Oh no," laughed the giant. "Oh no! Not at all! Someone wise in his own way. A giant dear to me—Pryat. You have seen my drawing of him. I will tell you more about him someday. You would be as friends, I know. Friends with *spinning heads*."

· TEN ·
Teleoscopes

Newton and Jat spent the next few months building their glass furnace, although all the heavy lifting was left to the giant. It grew from a section of the cliff face a fair distance from Newton's house, far enough, they hoped, to keep from burning down his home. A half dome of neatly stacked boulders formed a tight wall against the ledge. Worked into the stones of the inner wall was a granite shelf the width of a small barn. Even Newton had struggled with that one. The stone slab had to be rolled on its edge from a site over ten miles away. People at the most distant ends of the village felt the rumble beneath their feet. Hot firetide coal would be fed into the space beneath the platform. The sand, which would be melted into glass, would sit in a large stone basin on top.

When the last block had been laid, the two stood back and admired their work.

"You really know what you're doing," said Jat.

"Giants and stone are as brothers. We feel them. They are in us as if alive. Young giants are taught that we were all once stone before the Makers gave us life."

"Is that true?"

"Maybe yes. But again, maybe no. I often think the heads of some giants are filled with stones. But think about what we will make—this *glassss*. What is *glassss* but stones? Very small stones of sand made hot to stick together. It is inside this giant to make it."

"Well, I think you have room to make a lot of it. This furnace is huge. I could live in it."

"I would be happy to make another—a home for my friend," said Newton. "You could live more close to me."

"Maybe. Someday. I don't how much longer I'm staying here, though. For a little while, I know, but I think I might be moving on before next winter."

"Yes, to travel and to adventure. But, Jat? Can a prying giant ask a question you may not want a prying giant to ask?"

"No, he cannot. I don't know what it is, but if you put it that way, I know I won't want to hear it. So no."

"I am asking anyway," said Newton. "I know that the Fengiss brothers no longer pound you so much, and that is of a good thing. A good thing you made happen yourself. But I know, too, it is not over. They taunt you, still. They hurt you when they can, still. They drive others away, still. Is this why you wish to leave your—our—home?"

"They don't drive everyone away. I have other friends now. Or at least people who don't seem to hate me. Allander Quint, Sam Munken, Little Ran, Mason Twirp . . . Durd and

Sack don't bother me as much anymore. Maybe because they know I'll keep coming back after they knock me down. I think I'm tiring them out. They moved on to others now, like Allander, Sam, Little Ran, Twirp . . ."

"If you were to all join as one in battle, you might . . ."

"Don't you think we do? Not all of us, but sometimes a couple of us together make them back off. But sometimes that doesn't work out so great. I just don't talk to you about it because I don't want you helping me with this one," said the boy.

"Oh," huffed the giant, "but you let them help you, and this giant cannot?"

"It's more me helping them, Newton. I don't mind you helping me with things—we help each other all the time. Just not this, okay? We're the ones with the problem. It's a *peoples* thing. I can't let a giant fix it."

"Wait, Mason Twirp? Isn't he the . . ."

"Yeah, he's all right. I think he was just going along with Durd and Sack so he didn't get punched on himself. Which is exactly what happened when he stopped going along with them. I'm not running away from anything, Newton. I'm running *to* something, okay?"

"I do know of the dream awakened in my friend. You would be like Theobold the Explorer. Or Newton Big Ears."

"Of course you would come. Of course, right?"

"Of course, maybe," said the giant. "Of course, maybe not. You are my friend, and I can think of no better life. But I will soon be traveling far, too. Traveling more far than my walking boots can carry me. And my boots will never leave this sand."

"Staring through some great big tube isn't really traveling," said Jat.

"I have learned that to be different, Jat. A giant has a body. Yes?"

"Yes, a big one."

"Big to you, but not to me, or other giants. A giant has a mind. Yes?"

"Uh-huh."

"A body can travel with the mind asleep. A mind can travel with the body asleep." Newton paused, waiting for his friend to nod. "But the body," he continued, "can go only where its boots can take it. The mind, Jat, can travel to lands beyond the Makers. To *worlds* of lands, as Flora says. Far beyond a giant's boots."

Jat was silent a moment. "Okay," he said, "BUT can't a giant do both? Can't you just walk *and* look *and* think all at the same time? I do . . . sometimes. Or your body can travel, and then your mind can travel, and then your body can travel a little farther, and then your mind can catch up . . ."

Newton tilted his head, considering the question. "*Haroomph* . . . maybe," he said.

Winter passed, and then spring. By early summer the giant and the boy had reached the point where they could roll and stretch a piece of glass strong enough to hold its place in a framed wall opening. The trick was to get it to the right temperature to remove all the air bubbles. Fira's cottage was the first to be adorned with windows. "They are like eyes in my home," she said. "It feels like they're looking at me. And I can see myself in them." She leaned in for a closer look and then grimaced.

"*Uhhk*. That is my mother looking at me!"

"You don't like them?" asked Jat.

"I don't know . . . I'll get used to it." Fira leaned in closer to the glass and ran her fingers down her cheeks. She shook her head and stepped away. "It *will* be brighter than the hides. Bugs can't fly through it?"

"It's glass, Mother. Like Grandmother's chalice. Nothing can get through it. But it is easy to break, so be careful."

"I'll get used to it . . ."

In time, there was enough glass for anyone who wanted it, and nearly everyone did. All Newton asked in payment was a story. It could be any story. The giant was hungry to learn as much about his people as he could. Some stories made it onto his *talking wall*, which is what he now called the ever-expanding mural on the cliff face.

Jat, against Newton's wishes, brought a few panes to Abner Willowhock. The giant told him that the Willowhock was not a good mans. What he made, he made for good mans and womans—good *peoples*. Not for makers of problems. Not for cursers of babies' nurses.

"And he will not take it," he added. "He will demand his *fo fum* ox cows."

"I'm just trying to end this," said Jat.

"So you are trying to help this giant with his trouble with another mans? *Hrmmmmph* . . . What does this sound like, this giant wonders . . ."

"It's different, Newton."

"*No, it is not*," mumbled the giant.

Abner Willowhock's fences had long been repaired and a new herd of calves grazed in his field. Their flanks bore a brand in the shape of an *X*.

"Why did you change your circle-*W* brand?" asked Jat.

"Never yeh mind. What be this?" he asked, eyeing the glass in the boy's cart. "Ice?"

"It's a gift from Newton. He made this for you. *We* made it. You can put it in the holes in your walls so you can let the light in and keep the wind and rain and snow out. Your place won't be so dark anymore, on the inside. Also keeps the flies out. You have a LOT of flies here—a *real* lot of flies . . . You just have to make a wooden frame for it to hold in place . . ."

Willowhock had a closer look.

". . . which I'm sure you know how to do," continued the boy.

"Those don't look like cows to me."

Jat buried his face in his hands. "AGHH!" he shouted in frustration. He pointed to the corral. "You have cows again— well, calves . . . *Probably someone else's*," he added under his breath. "Do you want this, Mr. Willowhock? It's a gift. We're making peace. Or, as Newton would say, he's honoring his take-give, or something like that."

Willowhock lifted the panes from the cart and held them to his face. The distortion in the glass soured further his already soured features. He smashed the windows to the ground, shattering two days' worth of work at his feet.

"Cheap work. They break too easy. I won't be acceptin'," he said, and returned to his house.

When not making windows for the villagers, the giant worked on the waterstones for his farlooker. This took far more time and precision than the comparatively simple process of rolling out flat sheets of glass. Through trial and error, he learned that slight adjustments in the curvature and thickness of the glass added to its performance. Jat had suggested that instead of using a hollow log to join the two "eyes," as he called them, they could ask Mynar Blodge, a woodworker, to build him something better. Mynar was happy to do it.

"How could I not," he said. "Those walnut trees from the hills you brought me? Best wood in the land! Dark grain. Tough as iron."

While he didn't quite understand what he was making, in a few weeks he had constructed a thirty-foot-long cylindrical tube to hold the waterstones at both ends. The tube consisted of long wooden staves, held together, barrel-like, with copper straps. Fenton Quigley, the town's blacksmith, attached it to the top of a heavy wooden chair with a curved iron arm. Beneath the chair he had made a pivoting brace that allowed Newton to swivel to any point in the sky by moving his feet on the platform.

Newton's nights were spent among the stars. He was traveling again, as he had back home. This farlooker, however, was by far superior to the first. His mind flew through swirling clouds of glowing suns, tails of streaming skyfire, colorful bursts of countless stars, seemingly frozen in mid-explosion. The giant, the largest being in the land, felt smaller than what made up a single grain of sand beneath his boots. At times, it made the sizzling pain inside him seem smaller yet. What was a giant's pain in a sky so big? He was happy.

The Fire Sea glowed offshore, as it always did. Newton

suspected its light could be fading the images in the night sky, much in the way a candle's flame seems brighter in the dark than under the light of the sun. *Would I see more up there if it were more dark down here?* He would build another and find out. *I can make* many *more for many places*, he thought. He liked that thought so much he thought it again and again.

The giant also searched the Fire Sea itself. It was still a mystery to him, and to his fellow villagers, it seemed. Jat, and others, said that it was surrounded on both sides by an ocean of salt water. No one had ever traveled through the flames themselves—no one could, except for him, of course. Once. But likely not again. *Theobold found a way around it. At least his boooks did.* Not that Newton wished to leave.

One morning, the giant rolled out from beneath the tele-oscope. He had fallen asleep under it, as he usually did. He climbed down the ladders and into the big open room of his home. He walked over to the window to another, smaller tele-oscope. He had made it for looking at the Fire Sea when it was raining. For a reason he did not yet understand, the smaller size allowed it to work better during the day. He trained it on the distant horizon and searched yet again for the twisting vines of water that had set him on the path to this land. Could he see other lands it led to? Maybe, if he found it, he could show others. Maybe they would know why it was there. *And what keeps it there . . .*

The orange-hued air shimmered in the heat, distorting the view. The horizon was a snaking wave, slithering across the land's end. Then, just at the edge of the farthermost lick of flame, he spotted something. At first he thought he had found the waterspout, but then another speck appeared, soon to be followed by three more. He pulled it away from his face and rubbed his tired eyes.

"This giant has worn his eyes down. Too long with no rest," he said to himself. But he brought the glass back to his eye. The flickering specks were still there and slowly growing larger. The sun rose higher in the sky, bringing into better view the distant shapes. Newton gasped and lurched back away from the eyepiece. Those were not specks. Those were not shapes. They were giants.

ELEVEN

The Stonehall Blunge

Newton raced to Jat's house, the pounding of his legs rattling the surrounding trees. He had to tell him what he'd seen. *But what can Jat do?* he wondered. *What can a boy do? What can a village of mans do?*

What can a giant do?

Nothing.

But he had to tell him. When he got there, Jat was gone. No one was home. The giant looked around and then clambered up the pile of firecoal next to the house. He couldn't see much more, looking down through the treetops.

"JAAAAT!" he bellowed. His voice carried for miles.

"What are you doing up there?" shouted the boy from below. "We were right down the path."

Mason Twirp was with him. He looked up at the giant, his knees shaking. The pug-nosed boy was slightly taller than Jat and seemed to have outgrown his clothes some time ago.

"I didn't . . . I wasn't," Twirp stammered. "We were going to town to get some pears from Mr. Derring. We . . ."

"He won't hurt you, Twirp. He knows we're friends now." Jat looked up at the giant. "Is something wrong? Your face looks like something is wrong."

"Come," said the giant. "We have to go fast." He looked at Jat's friend. "You can wait here, or go home."

"Wait a—" Jat started to say.

"JAT! NOW!"

"Okay, okay! Twirp, I'll see you later." But Mason Twirp was already a good ways down the path and out of sight.

"That wasn't—" began the boy.

"Get on my shoulder," said the giant.

"Are you sure? You never let me do that. Told me you're not a 'horse-ox.'"

"Just climb on. Do not argue." The giant bent down so Jat could climb up his arm and onto his shoulder. Then he stood up and tromped back toward his home.

"What . . . is . . . going . . . on?" asked the boy, his fingers wrapped tightly around the heavy threads of the giant's shirt.

"Giants. They're coming. They're here," said Newton.

They reached his home in short time. Newton clumped over to the teleoscope by the window. He picked it up and put the waterstone to his eye.

"What do you see?" asked Jat, still on his shoulder.

"Giants," said Newton. He put it down on the sill of the window. "Look."

Jat climbed down from his shoulder and walked up to the

telescope. The lens was wider than his face, but he could see something in the distance.

"I see three . . . four . . . five. Five somethings. Those are giants? How can you tell? Everything is so wavy. And they're so far away."

"They are giants," sighed Newton. "And they are coming for this one."

"Why is it so important? Or *you* so important? They fried you in lightning and then you got out of their way. What more can they want?"

"I do not know. But I do know they are here for me. It is not easy to get here, Jat. I do not know how they found me."

"They haven't found you yet, Newton."

Newton turned away from the window to look at the boy. He smiled. "No, Jat. They have not."

"So let's figure this out. Are you in danger?"

"Yes, Jat. They are not coming to watch me dance the Stonehall Blunge."

"You make your first joke ever, and it's now?"

"It is my regret," said the giant.

"Am *I* in danger? Are the people—my mother and sister—are *they* in danger, Newton?"

Newton considered this. "Yes, Jat. This giant thinks so. We should act as if you and they are."

"Okay," said Jat. "Give me a minute." He looked back through the lens. "They are really far. We have time. I think we can't keep this a secret, but I'm afraid that if we tell everyone, they will panic."

"So . . ."

"Wait a minute," said the boy, holding up his hand. He

was silent a moment. "I hate to do this, but I think we have to tell Constable Stoggin."

"This giant agrees," said Newton. "He is here to protect your peoples, and he should know from what."

"Back to town?"

"Yes."

"Do I get a ride?" asked Jat. The giant nodded. He bent over to let the boy climb up.

Back in the village, they spotted the constable across the green. He was in the middle of scolding Bonnie Mullein. He was often in the middle of scolding Bonnie Mullein.

"But why did you have to shove the pie in Grandy's face? You're a deputy now, not a ruffian. You already stopped him from stealing it. And now it's still as good as being stolen!"

"He wasn't sorry."

"And?"

"And what?"

"You could have stopped the thievery AND rescued Mrs. Whipny's pie. Without attacking a citizen. Two good things, you could have done. Instead, two bad things you . . . did you . . . do. YOU know what I mean!"

"But if he is sorry for what he did, then maybe I stopped him from doing *three* more bad things. At least that's what I was thinking."

"I don't think you were thinking at all . . ."

Newton and Jat bounded up to the keepers of peace, who were being anything but peaceful. Bonnie and Constable Stoggin spun around and looked up at the giant.

"Hey! What are you doing up there?" called Bonnie to Jat. "Can I come up?"

"No," said Newton. "And he's coming down." Newton reached up and gently grabbed the boy. He set him on the ground next to the other two.

"We need to talk," said Jat. "There's trouble. BIG trouble. And I mean big, BIG trouble."

"Let's hear it," said the constable.

Jat told them about the giants they'd seen in the Fire Sea. Newton assured them that their coming was "not of a good thing."

"What do they want with you?" asked Stoggin.

"This giant does not know for sure, but can guess. Back home, my old home, I learned of the lands and stars of the night sky. I have spoken of this here before. First I learned from *boooks*, and then I made a teleoscope, like the one back by the Fire Sea. A time came when skyfire fell—sent by the Makers' Dragon, or so they say."

"Sent by a soup spoon," said Jat.

Newton smiled half a smile. "Yes. The angry soup spoon." He turned back to the constable. "But it was neither. They are just stars. This giant has learned that stars can gather in many shapes that can look like other things. All other giants believe what they are told, that things that look like things *are* those things. And because of that, this giant was to be punished."

"This is taking a long time," said Bonnie.

"And we know about what they did to you," added Stoggin. "Are we going to get eaten by monsters from your world, or not?"

"Not monsters," said the giant. "The giants of my world believed that I angered the Makers when I looked up to their lands. They believe the skyfire is because of me. They believe one destroyed homes because of me."

"He doesn't burn," Jat added. "Giants don't burn, but their stuff does. Their homes and fields. Their forests."

"Yes. It can be bad. But it is not because of me. I have told them this, but they listen to their holygiants who say, 'Newton—no, *Broont*, this giant's old name—brings skyfire to our land and must go to the Makers. And that I must tell them I am of a regret. I must tell them I will not spy on them again."

"Did you?" asked Stoggin. "This IS taking a long time!"

"Yes. But this giant did not tell them those things. Because they are not of a truth. Instead, their lightning— their Voice—burned me inside. And does still. I escaped. I am here. They come."

"So you don't think they are finished with you?" asked Bonnie. "What will bringing you back do?"

"What if their skyfire was still flying around when they left?" asked Jat.

"That is what this giant believes. It has nearly ended here, so it would be the same there. But they would not be of this knowledge. It is a long journey from our land to this one. They would not have seen the change that happened not too long ago."

"So if they still think it's coming down there, then they might think they still need you to stop it," said Bonnie.

"Yes," said Newton.

". . . So here they come," said Jat.

Constable Stoggin listened quietly. Then no one spoke.

He paced in small circles, hands behind his back. His thick gray mustache puffed out with each breath.

"What if—" began Bonnie. Stoggin held up his hand to silence her. He paced some more.

Finally, he came to a stop and bent back to look up at the giant. He pointed a finger toward his face.

"I knew you were going to be trouble the day I met you. I knew it!"

"This giant is of a regret greater than you can know."

"Yeaaah . . . Okay, so this is what we are going to do. And I hate the thought of it, but we have to go to Ellery Manor."

"What good will that do?" asked Bonnie.

"Good? Probably none. Going there rarely gets anything *good* done. But we need to mobilize people. A lot of them. Most of them. And they are *his* people—well, we're at least people on *his* land. We all are. It would be better to get him with us now than to have him blunder in at the wrong time and send us nine steps backward."

"What do we need the people for?" asked Jat.

"An enemy gathers at the Fire Sea. We need to prepare to defend ourselves."

"We can get every single person in our village and it won't stop five of these," said Jat, pointing up to his friend. "It won't even stop one of them."

"Well, not trying to stop them won't stop them," said the constable. "We're going to Ellery Manor, and that's the all of it."

Newton nodded. On horseback, Ellery Manor was a three-hour full-out ride from the center of town. They didn't have that much time.

"This giant is a horse-ox again. Climb on."

"Are you serious?" asked Constable Stoggin. "Because if you are, I think a mountain fell on yer head! I'm goin' back and gettin' my Merit!"

"Not me!" said Bonnie. "I'm ridin' the giant! And Thumbridge brought Merit to be reshoed back at the barn."

"He walks fast," said Jat. "I don't think we have a lot of time." The giant lifted the boy onto his shoulder.

"Arrgh! I don't like it, giant. And I don't like you! You are trouble, and you—" His words cut off as Newton lifted him off the ground and tossed him, ungently, onto his other shoulder.

"You can continue to tell me how you do not like me," said the giant, "but let us move as you do." He picked up Bonnie and set her next to Jat. Jat smiled uncomfortably and looked away.

Newton bounded ahead to Ellery Manor with the endless berating of Constable Stoggin ringing in his ear.

TWELVE

Blackpoint Falls

"How does one hide a giant?" asked Lord Ellery. The tulip he held to his nose gave his pinched voice a slightly hollow ring.

Newton, Jat, Constable Stoggin, and Bonnie Mullein had made it to Ellery Manor in short time. A giant can take routes impossible to travel for even the most spry of horses. Upon seeing them, Lord Ellery tried to hide behind the archway that led to his home.

"HA! I see you!" shouted Bonnie from Newton's shoulder. The lord stepped out sheepishly from behind the arch. The group was reluctantly invited to join him in the courtyard. As sprawling as his manor was, it would not hold a giant.

Lord and Lady Ellery owned the land upon which they all lived. It had been in Lord Ellery's family for centuries. The land was home only to Jat's tiny village, too small to be of notice to the king on the mainland, whoever that was these days. They were left alone to fend for themselves and were content to do so. If the king, or queen—whoever was ruler of the land—didn't know they existed, he or she could not collect money from them. The lord left most of the daily decisions to the people, mostly because he didn't really care what they did, so long as they paid their land fees. On matters they could not resolve, Constable Stoggin would step in. If that didn't do it, and if he couldn't convince Lady Ellery to handle it, he'd uneagerly deal with it in as quick a fashion as possible. Anyone who disagreed with his final decision was free to leave. That was the law of the land. If you don't like it, leave. There were no jails or prisons. You were sent off, and that was the end of it. He had little patience for anything that took him away from his gardens. Lord Ellery spent nearly every waking moment tending his three hundred acres of tulips. He claimed he had created the most magnificently beautiful landscape in the world. No one could argue with him, though, since only he was allowed to set foot in it. Of course Lady Ellery would be granted permission, though she rarely cared to ask.

The lord, born Faunstice Hendrican Adelard Ellery, had grown up in the manor with his younger sister, Eularia. The siblings never shared a fondness for each other. He was always a bit of a jellyfish, and she a bit of a surly bear. As was the Ellery tradition, when the older sibling came of age, he or she took control of the manor and the attached village. The parents and younger siblings were expected to move out. Why this custom was in place had long been forgotten, but it was believed that breaking the tradition would end the long chain of good fortune the Ellerys had enjoyed.

Regardless of tradition, his parents, eager to separate themselves from their two offspring, had left for their summer villa years earlier. When the time came, his sister refused to go. Faunstice had his guards drag her out and deliver her to a modest estate on the edge of town. In time, the lord married a young woman named Arabella. That is all anyone knew about her—her name. She wasn't from the area, and it was rumored, although she never said it was so, that she came from the court of a larger kingdom far beyond their borders. Even her husband was kept in the dark as to her history. She maintained a regal bearing and was willing to run things for him. And was quite fetching. In Faunstice's eyes, those three qualities outweighed any concern he might harbor over her mysterious background.

Back at the edge of the village, Eularia married a butcher named Bartholomew Fengiss. He eventually grew tired of her overbearing nature and left, leaving behind their two boys, Durd and Sack.

In the courtyard of the manor, Jat contemplated Lord Ellery's question. "I don't know how to hide a giant," said Jat. "But we have to hide him. They are going to take him away and kill him."

"I do not want them to come here," said Newton. "They are not friendly like this giant. I will leave."

"Now you are making sense," said the constable.

"And what shall happen when they find you have taken to foot?" asked Lady Ellery. "Will they rend our village to tattered ribbons in search of you? I know of giants and what they can do."

"*My* village," corrected her husband.

"*Harooomph* . . . I do not know," said Newton. "Did you say you know of giants?"

"Only from . . . long ago, but that is not important now."

"Well, he can't stay here," said the constable. He looked up to Newton. "I'm sorry, fella. I have ta look after our folk. I will personally tell your big friends that you were here but left for the hills."

"He *is* our folk," said Jat, and then, to the giant, "Will that even work?"

"Thank you, Jat," whispered Newton loudly. "I do not know," he continued. "They risked their hides to come here. Their boots *crossed water*. They will not leave without this giant. You do not want them here. I know this more than I know anything. I will go to them and surrender."

"And they will kill you on that thorn thing," said Jat. "Wait! What if they see that your shooting stars aren't . . . shooting anymore? Would they call it off?"

"First I would have to make them believe it. I would not be able to do that until we returned and they saw it for themselves. And even then, they will send me to the Makers to answer for anything that may have happened while I was here. Or they will not. This giant does not know. But I do know as a truth that no words I speak would move them to leave without me."

"That's it, then," said Jat. "You have to hide. When they don't find you here, they'll keep looking somewhere else. There will be no reason for them to stay."

"Thorn thing?" asked Bonnie.

"It's real bad," said Jat.

"If they seek him and find him not, they will be irritable," said Lady Ellery.

"That is true," said Newton. "You do not want . . . *irritable* giants stomping around. One *peaceable* giant breaks enough things. They will bring Punchers, too. You do not want them here even more! I will go with them. I will not let them harm my friends."

"Those big tree things you told me about? The ones that beat up giants?" asked Jat.

"Yes. The ones that beat up giants," said Newton.

"That was easy enough," said Bonnie.

"What do you mean, 'easy enough'? You would sacrifice Newton to those giants?"

"It's his decision," said the girl. "I agree with Constable Stoggin. We have to look out for ourselves."

"I guess you're pretty good at that," said Jat.

"What is that supposed to mean?"

Jat frowned. "I don't even know."

"Not ourselves, Bonnie. Our people," corrected the constable.

"Same thing," she muttered.

Lady Ellery considered Newton's offer. "Who is to say they won't attack us after you relinquish yourself unto them?"

Newton thought a moment. "I cannot say that will not happen. I do not know how they will treat mans and womans. I cannot say they will eat you. But I cannot say that they will not."

"Well, *that's* great news," said Stoggin.

"They will at the least *feast* upon our livestock," said Lord Ellery, shooting Newton an accusing look. "You giants seem to like to eat people's cows. I've certainly heard enough about that from a certain someone."

Newton hung his head, ashamed. "That they will do. They will be hungry. It is my regret. It is my regret for all of this."

"You can stop saying that," said Jat. "We know."

"If the giants attack, we'll want a giant by our side," said the constable. "One giant would be better than none."

"This giant would do what he could," said Newton. "But it would not be much. I counted three giants and two Punchers."

"You are smarter than all of them combined," said Jat. "We have that."

Newton shrugged.

"Here's an idea, then," said Stoggin. "Let's say we hide you. If they give up and move on, you're—*we're*—okay. But if they threaten us, then you give yourself up. If they still threaten us after that, well . . ."

"Well what?" asked Lord Ellery.

"We fight."

"You fight, you lose," said the giant.

The group was silent a moment. There seemed to be no solution that would guarantee safety for Newton or the town. No one could guess how the villagers would be viewed by a troop of angry giants.

Bonnie punched her hand. "Ha! I know where we can hide a giant AND a village!"

"Can't wait to hear this, girl," said Stoggin.

"How many people are there in the village?"

Lord Ellery closed his eyes as he counted on his fingers. "Four hundred and . . ."

"Three hundred and fifty-eight," said Lady Ellery. Her husband eyed her suspiciously. She returned his gaze. "It's a number you should know as well, my lord. I would wager you know exactly how many of those meretricious weeds you bend knee to. Newton, how long do you believe we have until they make arrival?"

"They will be here by morning," he said. "Maybe tonight, but they will be tired. They will need to rest. To eat . . ."

"Blackpoint Falls!" said Jat. "The cavern behind the waterfall! It's hidden behind the water. It can hold all of us, including this great beast!" The giant met the boy's smile with furrowed eyebrows.

"Yep," said Bonnie. "You're a little slow, but you catch up."

"Could work," said the constable. "I've seen it. Plenty big—used to play there as a child. Problem is getting everyone there. It's a half day's slog. And that's for the young and healthy. Not everyone has horses, either. What about the rest?"

"Half a day for mans and womans, maybe," said Newton. "Faster for a giant. I can bring those who cannot walk there. I can carry them. Falling waters is good. It will hide us from their noses, too. But you cannot bring your horse-oxes. A tasty horse-ox is easy to smell, maybe even through water; many tasty horse-oxes, more easy to smell."

"You eat horses, too?" asked Lord Ellery disgustedly.

"This giant does not, though they smell like ox cows. They are your pets. And I like them a great much as so. The other giants . . . yes, they would eat them."

"Could we not convey our elders and infirm upon our

timber wagons? Each should hold about twenty souls. How many could you carry?" asked Lady Ellery.

"I will carry as many as I must. The giants will leave once they have eaten your food. When they do, we come back. They will look for me in other places. They may know of a way to return home. They must if they are here to bring me back. If they do not know I am here, they may leave."

"We would need to keep a watch out for them until they're gone for good," said Jat.

"So, we move an entire village on the word of a single man . . . giant?" asked the lord.

"I believe him," said Lady Ellery. "And more so, I trust Constable Stoggin. If he believes this to be true, I am of no doubt that it is."

"I haven't seen it myself," said the constable, staring up at Newton, "but call me a mule-kicked fool, I don't think he's making this up. Are we doing this? This is our plan?"

They all looked to Lord Ellery. He looked to his wife, who nodded.

Ellery let out a breath, blowing a petal from the tulip. "I so decree."

"It's going to take a while to get everyone together," said Stoggin.

"I will get them to the circle," said the giant. "My voice is loud. All will hear."

Upon their return, Newton's voice rumbled throughout the village, calling all mans and all womans at once to the town circle. Their lives were in danger. He hoped they would see this. In short time, a large crowd had gathered, anxiously waiting to find out the reason for their summoning. Lord and Lady Ellery, who rarely visited their village, did so this time. Lady Ellery explained the trouble they were in and the solution they'd come up with. Everyone was to go back to their homes and return with three or four days' worth of food. Small parties could be sent back to town to sneak more supplies to the cave if needed later. Those too weak to travel would ride with the giant. Pets, horses, and all livestock should be set free, giving them a better chance to evade the ravenous appetites of the invaders. The surviving animals would be rounded back up later, when the danger had passed. Several young men and women would be dispatched to share this news with the people who were not there. They would leave before sunset and hoped to arrive at the falls in the middle of the night. Those who could leave sooner, should.

"I know this is a lot for you to do when at present all seems at peace," she finished. "We are telling you to pick up and flee when you have seen nothing from which to flee. But trust me. Trust *us*. Giants are coming. I know not how they got past the swirl, but they are coming." She pointed to Newton. "He and the boy have laid eyes upon them. Constable Stoggin trusts their word, as do the lord and I. If we do not hide until they move on, we give our lives up to foolishness." Lady Ellery turned to her husband. "Would you add anything?"

He pursed his lips. "No," he answered. "That was good."

Newton bent down to the lady. "The *swirl*? You know of this?"

Lady Ellery looked uneasy. "Did you not speak of it?"

To you? Maybe, but also maybe not, thought Newton.

Some in the crowd began to argue. How did the giant know they were in danger? What if the giants chose to bypass this village? Fennelstock was just a three days' journey; maybe they would head there. It was a much larger village.

Eularia Fengiss stepped forward. "Why not put us all up in your lofty palace? Or do you need the whole thing for you and your lady to hide in? And how can we trust this monster who threatened to eat my children?"

Jat looked across the crowd at Durd and Sack, giving them a threatening scowl. The two brothers feigned a look of innocence.

"This giant alone could tear it down with great ease. It would not hold," said Newton. "And I did not threaten to eat any mans, ever!"

"We are going to the falls, too, Eularia," said Lady Ellery.

"We are?" asked her husband.

"I am. As are you," she answered.

"We do not have time to second-guess," bellowed Constable Stoggin. "I am charged with your safety, and I believe this is our only hope. If you don't trust me, then stay. The giants who come are hungry. They'll be more than happy to bite off the heads of each and every one of you they catch." He pointed up to Newton. "Imagine something even bigger than this slovenly beast shoving you in its rotting mouth! It's not a good way to go, and we can't stop it. We will NOT stand around and debate this. Get your things. Return at sunset. Go now! We may all get through this with our heads still attached."

Newton bent over to the constable. "I did not say—" he began.

Bonnie jabbed his toe with her spear. "Shh!" she whispered. "You want them to come, don't you?"

"Slovenly, though? Rotten?"

The crowd broke up, muttering loudly.

"They may not all come back," said Stoggin to Lord Ellery.

"I did what I could," said the lord. His wife rolled her eyes.

Most of the villagers did return, each heavily laden with what they'd need to survive a few nights in the cavern. Some, who knew where they were going, had already set out for the falls. They had correctly reasoned that if there could be one giant, others might exist. And they trusted their constable. This could be a very real threat. Newton heaved the two heavy wagons, each carrying twenty-one people, onto his shoulders. The wagons were connected by a thirty-foot yoke and dangled precipitously above the crowd. It was far more weight than he could handle, but he somehow found the strength. He had put them in danger just by being here. He would do everything in his power, and beyond, to keep them safe.

"Don't you be dropping us," shouted Flora.

"Will . . . not . . . happen," grunted the giant, and off they went.

They arrived at the falls by midevening, although many were there already. It had taken the main group longer than expected due to the darkness and slower members of the party. Jat led them along a narrow, rocky trail that disappeared behind the roaring veil of water. A few grumbled about getting wet, but that was to be expected, the complaining. Most found it difficult to imagine the real danger they were in. It was easier to complain about little things. And they were exhausted, none more than Newton, though. Forty-two mans are a heavy load.

Several brave men and women, the fastest sprinters, stayed behind at different points along the way. They would keep an eye out for the invaders. Bonnie took the post closest to the cave. She was the fastest runner out of all of them, and if the giants got that far, it would mean it was almost too late. The rest sat huddled in the cavern. There was just enough room for them, including the fifty-foot giant. Lady Ellery squeezed through the crowd, counting how many had made it.

"Three hundred forty-one, three hundred forty-two, three hundred forty-three . . . Almost all of us, including the runners we left behind."

"The Peregrins told me they were going to wait it out in their root cellar," said one of villagers. "That would make three hundred forty-seven."

"Stal Werthy and his son are away hunting," said another.

"The Millers are visiting family in Fennelstock," called out a voice from the back. "And my neighbor's doing the root cellar thing, too."

"Has anyone seen my sister-in-law and her family?" asked Lady Ellery. No one answered.

"That would be three hundred fifty-four. Who else is missing?"

· THIRTEEN ·
A Balance Made

Jat awoke at first light. He quickly scanned the faces of the people in the cavern. Most in the small village knew one another by sight. Candles helped them find their way around, but Newton cautioned them about burning too many, as the smell could give them away even behind the water. The boy pushed through the crowd, searching every face from the entrance at the waterfalls to the dark recesses in the back of the cave.

"Lose something?" asked Jern Baker. He and his family sat against the wall, all looking more annoyed than frightened.

"Not something; someone. Have you seen Mr. Willowhock?"

"I'm happy to say that I have not," said the man.

Mason Twirp grabbed the boy's shoulder. "Hey, Jat. Are you really sure about this?"

"That they're coming? Yeah. That this will work? No. But listen, I need your help. I have a bad feeling Mr. Willowhock is not here. And for a reason. Can you grab Little Ran and go through the crowd and see if he's here? It's dark, and I might have missed him. You know what he looks like?"

"Yeah, like a dusty old raven. I'll let you know if we find him."

Jat went through the crowd again. He met up with Twirp and Little Ran.

"He's not here," said Twirp.

"You know who else is not here?" asked Little Ran.

"Yeah, Durd and Sack. I'd be surprised if their mother and them came."

"Glad they didn't," said Twirp. "Well, mostly glad, I guess . . ."

Jat returned to the entrance. Newton sat quietly, leaning against the opening, his plump fingers playing in the spray of the falls. He chose to stay here to give the people more room inside, or so he told them. They didn't need to know how he felt about caves.

"Abner Willowhock didn't come," said the boy.

"I am not too sad about that, Jat," said the giant.

"I think maybe you should be. Not sad, but worried. What if he tells the other giants where we are?"

Newton gasped. "He would do that?"

"I don't know. He might," said the boy. "He really doesn't like you. I mean *really*. And Lord Ellery wasn't going to do anything about you. I wonder if he thinks he found some help that will. I'm gonna go back and find him. If he leads the giants to us, we are all trapped."

"This is my problem," said Newton. "I will go. I travel faster."

"I'll come with you, then. I can ride on your shoulder. If something happens to you, I'll run back and try to warn the others."

"Okay. Hurry and tell Fira you are leaving."

"It would be better if I didn't," said Jat.

"It would be better if you did, or this giant will be blamed."

"No time," said Jat. "Get me up there. Let's go!"

The giant and the boy left their hiding place and raced toward Willowhock's farm on the edge of the Fire Sea. "What if he's already told them?" asked Jat.

"It is of no help to think the worst, my friend."

But the worst was here. Just as they topped the hill on the other side of Willowhock's ranch, Jat picked out the party of giants on the beach.

"Get down!" he warned Newton.

Newton dropped to his belly, sending Jat rolling onto the ground.

"My regret," he whispered loudly. Newton squinted his eyes, trying to make out the individuals milling about in the sand. They looked battered down and ready to drop. They must have arrived in the middle of the night. He remembered making that same march beneath the flames of the Fire Sea. They would be hungry, too.

"What are those big tree things? The clobberers?" asked Jat.

"Punchers," said Newton. "I told you about them. They are like your—our—Constable Stoggin. Except they are not kind like him."

"I wouldn't call Constable Stoggin kind."

"You would if you met a Puncher. I will not be able to stop them." Then he remembered how Pryat had taken one down at the Iron Thorn. "A good-sized boulder, maybe . . ."

"Do you know the others?"

"Crag. He tells himself he is more than he is. He is an Elder of the Council. We are not as friends."

"So he is old? You can beat him, right?"

"Old does not mean weak to a giant, Jat. And he is a young elder, not very old. *Maybe* this giant can thrump him."

"Maybe? You can't *maybe* thrump. We can't lose this, Newton."

Newton pounded his chest with his fist, instantly reminding himself of the Makers' Voice smoldering inside him. It was worse than it had ever been. He winced in pain but shook it off. What he could not escape, though, was the thick feeling in the back of his neck. It was similar to when he turned. *But I cannot be turning. This giant is not of a turning fear.*

"It's still maybe," he said. "The hairless one, this giant does not know. Marlite is the female. She is a holygiant who works with the Council. You have seen her on my talking wall. We were . . . as friends when we were young giants. We are not now."

"That's a lady giant? She's no beauty, is she?"

Newton turned to the boy, a puzzled look on his great face. "I don't know. I think she could be of a beauty. Most giants would." He paused a moment. "Her nose could be more bigger, I would suppose . . ."

"There's Mr. Willowhock!" Jat pointed to the hillside across from them. Abner Willowhock was working his way down a narrow dirt trail, several of his cows in tow. "He *is* going to give us away! Those cows are for the giants."

"As you knew he would, Jat," said the giant. "All mans should listen to you when you are of a thought."

"I know," said the boy.

Newton stood. Willowhock would have heard their plan. He might have even been in the circle when it was announced. *How can one be of so much hate? He would put his people in danger just to make me pay for his bony ox cows!* He knew there was just one thing left for him to do. It would likely bring his journey to an end, but it would save his friends, he hoped. He turned to Jat.

"Go back to the falls," he said. "I will not let him tell the giants where we hide. I do not know what they will do to our friends. Jat, I did not say this before, but . . . I do believe they might think mans are food."

"You kind of did say that was possible, Newton. What about you?"

"No, mans are not food for this giant. And it is a thing that you know! Stop this!"

"NO! I KNOW that! What are *YOU going to do*?"

"Oh. I will make them chase me." He pointed toward the sea and drew a line across the air. "There, along the shore. Then up into the western hills, far from any village. They will follow. What will happen then, will happen then, as all that happens does."

"They will catch you is what will happen then," said the boy.

"Maybe yes. But again, maybe no. If I live, I will come to the falls to tell you it is safe to return home. If I do not come in three days, then . . . thank you for being my first and last friend here. I wish your boots to grow worn with travels and adventures."

"Not without you. See you in *three* days, Newton. *Three* days, or sooner!"

The giant smiled through his glistening eyes. He would miss his friend. He gave a big sniff and clumped down the hill and up the other side toward Willowhock. In just a few great strides, he reached the rancher and scooped him up in his hand. The giants down by the firetide saw their quarry. *They will not be returning without me now*... The giants gathered what was left of their strength and lumbered after him. *Good*, thought Newton, *they look almost too tired to move.*

"Put me down!" shouted the rancher.

"So the Willowhock can betray his own people? You are coming with me," said Newton.

"Where? Put me down!" shrieked Willowhock. He chewed on the giant's finger, but Newton felt nothing. He lifted him to his face. He was angry, and it showed very much. Willowhock stopped fighting. His body went limp with fear.

"I should EAT you," snarled the giant. "I should bite you in half like your *fo fum* ox cows. Or maybe just bite off your legs and throw you into the Fire Sea. But I promised you a balance, and a giant always makes his balance. I will let you live. I took your ox cows. I give you your life. Now we have balance. No. Now you owe ME balance!"

Willowhock's face turned white. He said nothing. Newton stomped along the coast. The three giants were far behind, too tired to keep up. One of the Punchers, though, seemed in better shape. For every step Newton took, the Puncher's long legs covered the distance in half a stride. *Only one Puncher? Where's the other one?*

Newton turned away from the Fire Sea and cut up into a thick copse of firs. Many of the trees were taller than his ample height, and he hoped they would help conceal him from his pursuers. He needed his hands to push through. Time to get rid of his prisoner. He set Abner Willowhock atop a sixty-foot spire.

"You are many miles from troublemaking," he said. "Do not call for help. Trust this giant's words. You will not like the help that comes. You have nothing for them now but a way to fill a small space in one of their bellies."

Willowhock wrapped his arms and legs around the prickly branch, hanging on for life.

"Yeh be a cruel monster," he spat. "I hope they catch yeh! I hope they rip yer arms off! I hope they make yeh eat yer own glass, bite by bite by spittin' bite!"

Newton was about to answer but instead gave the tree a quick shake. Willowhock squeaked like a mouse, scrambling to keep from being thrown. The giant smiled and pushed through the dense forest.

In time, the trees thinned out. The Fire Sea was now a distant glimmer from the top of the mountain. He kept checking to see if he was followed, but he did not see the Puncher. *Maybe they went back to eat the Willowhock's ox cows?* Newton sat on the snow-powdered rocks to figure out his next move. He was sure he had lured the giants away from the village. Even if they did stop to eat, it would be quick, and they'd be right back after him in this direction. Anything that happened to him from now on he would greet boots to boots. He kept buried the pain from the Makers' Voice. It threatened to overtake him when he was distracted. *Too much to do. This will not stop me.* He noticed that his arms and legs had been growing stiff. His skin was harder than usual, as if he had come out of a turning, or was just entering it. But he wasn't turning. *Too much to do. This will not stop me.*

The cold air turned his breath into a fog that hugged the mountaintop. He turned and looked down behind him into a deep ravine. It dropped so far, he could not see the bottom. There was no way for him to climb down. He'd have to skirt the edge and push through the trees down the other side. The problem was, his pursuers would find it very easy to track him from atop this mountain. He had no choice, though.

"Giants chase. Newton runs. And so it goes." He let out a deep sigh, sending his steaming breath down the crest of the peak. A shadowy gray figure emerged from the fog. It was the Puncher called Greyelm. Newton was about to take a step back but caught himself just before going over the edge of the great drop. He had nowhere to go. He picked up a boulder and hurled it at the huge giant. It bounced harmlessly off the Puncher's chest. *Fum! It worked for Pryat.* The Puncher's face showed no emotion. It didn't smile. It didn't frown. There was no anger or hatred. It was given a task, and it would stay with that task until it was finished.

"You fight for the wrong side," said Newton. "The Apooncha serve us well, but not this time. Newton is not your enemy. *Broont* is not your enemy."

The Puncher reached out and grabbed Newton's shoulder. The giant tried to wrench free, but Greyelm's grip was too strong. It raised a fist the size of Newton's head and smashed him in the face. The giant's knees buckled. He reached toward the Puncher, trying to wrap his arms around its waist. The Puncher struck again, this time knocking its captive unconscious. It let go of Newton, allowing him to fall to the ground. Its task complete, it sat and waited for the other giants to catch up.

· FOURTEEN ·
Constable Stoggin

Jat raced back to Blackpoint Falls to warn the townspeople that the giants had landed. He was a fast sprinter, having raced the firetide since he was eight years old. He passed three of the runners stationed along the trail and waved them off when they tried to take their turn.

"Wait . . . for . . . giants," he told each one as he flew by them. He was beginning to slow down by the time he reached Bonnie, the last runner on the line. Jat quickly told her what he'd seen.

"You have to tell the others," he said.

"Are they bigger than our giant?" she asked.

"One of them is. The others are about the same size. One's a girl giant who has magic or something. And then there are those Puncher things. They're almost twice his size."

"And he got all but one to chase him. Okay. What do I tell them to do?"

"Just stay in the cavern. Put out all the candles—giants can smell things better than they can see or hear, but he said the water helps block it. Have someone keep watch to give warning. If that Puncher thing comes, and I think it will, I don't think it can fit inside."

"How do you know it will come?" asked Bonnie.

Jat pointed to the path leading to the waterfall. It looked as if a small village and a giant had plowed through.

"Kind of easy to follow our trail, I'd think. And again, they can smell things real good. They're like hunting dogs, but with much bigger noses. You better go. If you have time, run back here. The other runners will let you know when they see them. Then you should all get in the cavern. Blow out the candles. And keep quiet."

"What about you?"

"I'm going to head back to town. I think the big tree monster stopped off there to find food. Newton said they'd be starving. That's the one I'm worried about finding its way here. Someone has to keep an eye on it so we know where it is."

"How about me? I'm faster than you."

"No you're not," said Jat.

"You know I am."

"Okay, maybe, but let's stick to the plan. The faster you get back and warn the people, the better."

"Be careful, Jat," said the girl. She reached out and touched his shoulder, a look of concern on her face. "This is real, isn't it. Like you said . . ." The boy blushed.

"Hurry," he croaked. Bonnie took off down the trail. Jat watched her a moment. He let out a sigh and raced back toward the village.

The Puncher was easy enough to find. It clomped through the town, making no effort to avoid trampling homes and buildings as it searched for food. It found Wethcrall's sheep first. He had ignored the order to set them loose and put them in the barn prior to leaving for the falls.

"They're clever ones," he'd told Thumbridge. "They know when to keep quiet." Unfortunately, quiet as they were, they were easily discovered once that barn was kicked over on its side. Four sheep disappeared down the Puncher's throat in a gulp. Another three ran but were quickly scooped up to join the clever but unlucky flock.

Jat hid behind a tree. He was small enough to go unnoticed by the giant. Then he heard a shout. He looked up the hill and saw Sack waving frantically from under a wagon. Jat checked the Puncher, who was still kicking over buildings, and rushed to his lifelong enemy. He ran across the gravel road and dove under the wagon.

"What are you doing here? Where're your mother and brother?"

"I don't know!" said Sack. "What is that thing?"

"A kind of giant. A mean one. One that would *really* eat you, Sack. You need to get to the falls. Or go hide in the woods."

"I gotta find Durd and my ma!"

"Where did you last see them?"

Sack backed out from under the wagon. Jat followed. He turned around and sat down against the wooden wheel. Tears flowed from his eyes as he pointed up the hill toward his home. But there was no home there. Nothing was there.

"Oh," said Jat. "Um . . . there's nothing we can do now. You have to go hide so you can look for them later. I'm sure they might be okay."

"I'm not," cried the boy. "That thing crushed it into the ground!"

"I'm sorry, Sack. But I need to go back. Go hide, or come with me. I have to go warn everyone."

"I'm staying."

"Bad idea, but I gotta go," said Jat. He darted back across to the tree he had been hiding behind earlier. He watched as Sack left the cover of the wagon and ran up the hill toward what was left of his home. The Puncher saw him and started toward the boy. Sack turned, looked up, and screamed. Jat looked around him. Somehow, a pane of glass from one of the buildings sat, unbroken, on the ground.

"I think I made that one," he said to himself. He picked up the glass and smashed it against a large wooden door lying next to it. It exploded with a loud *CRIISSHH*! The Puncher stopped and turned at the sound. It headed toward him, kicking over a few more barns along the way. Then it stopped once again, sniffed the air, and froze. It turned its furrowed head toward the trail from which Jat had just come.

"Uh-oh," whispered the boy. He looked back toward Sack, who had resumed making his way up the hill.

The Puncher straightened and strode toward the path.

"That thing will get there before Bonnie! I wish you didn't leave this one behind, Newton!"

The Puncher walked toward the boy. Jat shrank behind

the tree. He wasn't much bigger than the monster's little finger. As soon as it stepped past him, he came out from hiding and leaped onto the back of its foot. Its hide was so riddled with cracks and ridges, it was easy to find hand- and footholds. Jat hung on for dear life. Each step lifted him fifteen feet in the air before crashing to the ground, the impact nearly knocking the boy loose. He dug his fingers so deeply into the giant's husk, the jarring tore off three of his fingernails.

The Puncher and the boy barreled down the trail, covering ground in less than half the time it had taken he and Newton earlier. They whisked past three of the runners, and then Bonnie, who had returned to her station after warning the villagers.

"She told them," he said under his breath. "Please be inside, everyone . . . Mother . . . Abby . . ."

They reached the base of the waterfalls. Jat dropped down to the ground and ran, quietly as he could, into the surrounding woods. He used the trees for cover as he moved around in a circle, closer to the entrance. A clap of thunder boomed in the distance, followed by several more. The rumbling went on and on, but there wasn't a cloud in the sky. The giant looked toward the noise. The boy took that moment of distraction to make his move, and he scuttled along the rocks at the base of the falls. He stole a last look at the Puncher, who was still staring toward the source of the thunder, and slipped into mouth of the cavern.

He was greeted by Bill Mullein.

"Did you see my daughter?" he asked.

"Yes," said Jat. "She's okay. She made it back to the trail." Then, to everyone, "You all saw what's here! Move to the back of the cave. Far as you can. I don't think it can fit." Fira emerged from the crowd and threw her arms around her son.

"Why do you always have to be in the middle of everything?" she asked.

"Mother, we have to push to the back! Go back, everyone!"

The people began to panic. The worried murmurs grew louder. Some wanted to have a peek at the giant. Lord Ellery stepped forward.

"Silence! Do as he says," he yelped. The crowd didn't move. If anything, they grew louder and more restless.

"It can hear us," said Jat to Lord Ellery. "The waterfall will only hide so much noise."

Constable Stoggin squeezed through the crowd and turned to face them. He held his spear sideways, using it to push back the frightened mass. Thumbridge did the same.

"You heard what he said," Stoggin whispered loudly. "MOVE BACK! NOW! IT'S HERE!"

That did it. Everyone backed as far as they could into the darkness of the cavern. Moments later, a dark gray silhouette appeared in the falls. Everyone froze and then piled back even farther, nearly crushing those against the wall. The Puncher's head pushed through the water, its dripping visage filling the opening of the cavern. Lifeless eyes, black as iron skillets, searched the shadows. It sniffed.

"Can it smell us?" whispered Fira.

"I don't know," Jat whispered back. "Probably."

The face retreated. Suddenly an arm shot through the cavity. A rough hand scraped the floor, then the walls, then the ceiling of their sanctuary. Someone, it was too dark to tell whom, was too close to the entrance. He, or she, was dragged out screaming. Crying was heard from the crowd. Then desperate shushing. All became silent again.

"How does one bring battle to such a thing?" whispered Lord Ellery. "Boy, you spend more time with that giant than anyone. Have you no knowledge of how to best this beast?"

Jat buried his face in his hands. "I'm thinking . . ."

A crash was heard outside. It shook the whole cave.

"You a slow thinker or a fast thinker?" asked Constable Stoggin.

Jat looked up. "I know that giants turn to stone when they are startled—or scared."

"Even the Apooncha? Are you certain?" asked Lady Ellery.

"No, I'm not, but Newton said it's a kind of giant."

Another crash rattled the villagers.

"Well, startled or scared, then?" asked Stoggin. "Which is it? They're two different things."

"I don't know," said the boy. "They're kind of the same. Aren't they?"

"Did I see what I think I saw from the entrance?" asked the constable. "Were you riding on its foot?"

"Yes, sir. I think we're too small for them to feel us. Or their bark, or skin, is too thick."

Abeleena, who had been clinging to Fira's skirts, spoke up.

"I can't tickle Newton 'cause my fingers are too small."

"Shh," shushed her brother.

"Shh yourself," said Stoggin. He rubbed his stubbly chin. "Remember, kid, how I tried to stop that giant, the first one—*Newton*—from coming to our village? You remember that?" Jat looked down guiltily. Stoggin turned back to the crowd. "Remember that, Flora? Well, I told you. Now I have to clean up this mess."

"What are you going to do, Father?" asked Thumbridge.

Stoggin turned to his son. "Boy, you are acting constable if something happens to me. Okay, Ellery?"

"Er . . . but . . ." said the lord.

The constable looked imploringly to Lady Ellery. She nodded.

"It's either you or Bonnie, boy," he said to his son. "Budge is useless. Sorry, Budge."

"No, it's okay. I really am," said the young deputy.

"What is going to happen? What are we going to do?" asked Thumbridge.

"Me, not we," said Stoggin.

CaaRASH! CRAASH! RUUUUMBLE . . . CRASH! The giant was tearing the mountain apart. Rocks tumbled down from the walls inside. Dust filled the air.

"Did this once or twice as a little one. Let's see if I can do it again," said the constable, his voice a little shaky. He removed his boots and bounced up and down, stretching his bowed knees.

"What are you—" began Lord Ellery, but Constable Stoggin was already running toward the entrance. He leapt into the falls and was swept into the bright light of the day. The Puncher, busy pounding on the side of their hiding place, did not notice the escape. Jat ran to the edge of the falls before his mother could stop him and peeked out from the wall of water. Thumbridge appeared behind him and pulled the boy back. He squeezed forward and took Jat's place. The deputy watched his father clamber up the side of the rock ledge near the giant. The giant was too busy to notice him. Stoggin crept along the boulders, keeping low, until he was just a few feet away from the towering creature.

"Does being wet block it from smelling him?" asked the deputy.

"Don't know," said Jat. "I hope so."

Thumbridge saw what his father was doing. "Over here!" he shouted. The Puncher turned. The constable leapt onto the back of its head and scrambled up to its ear. The giant appeared unaware of its passenger. It directed its attention to the young man and turned back toward the mouth of the cavern. With surprising speed, its arm shot out to grab Thumbridge and Jat. They were both yanked back out of reach by a pair of unseen hands.

"Careful, Scarecrow," said Budge.

"You can move fast when you need to," said Thumbridge.

"With you and Bonnie gone, I'd be next in line for your job. Not going to happen!"

"Bonnie's not gone," said Jat. "She's back . . ." Before he could finish his sentence, the Puncher's hand reached out again and snatched Budge from the edge of the cavern. All heard the chilling screams of terror as the baker's son was dropped into the giant's mouth.

"Push back now!" ordered Thumbridge. The two dove into the cowering crowd pressed into the rear of the cave. The giant's sinewy arm pushed back in, feeling for someone, someone to eat. They were all out of reach.

"We cannot do this forever," whimpered Lord Ellery. His wife held him and patted his forehead consolingly.

The arm receded. The Puncher stood back, studying this challenge. Constable Stoggin held on tight to the ridge that formed its outer ear. The giant slammed its fist into the wall, causing an avalanche of stone to rain down past the mouth of the cave. Stoggin was knocked loose and rolled down onto its shoulder. The creature stood up straight, studying the damage. Then it turned and sniffed the air, as if noticing a new smell. It stopped sniffing and returned its attention to the opening of the cave. It was still unaware of its tiny rider. The constable slowly scaled the neck and pulled himself up along the ridge of its ear. He reached up and grabbed the fold at the top and hung down. A dark and cavernous canal loomed before him. Mites the size of tortoises fed on the waxy deposits lining the walls. Stoggin tried to quiet his breathing to avoid giving himself away. His feet splayed out side to side, locking him in place. A mite crawled up his leg and he kicked it free. The monster pounded at the wall again. This knocked loose the rocks above the entrance, making the opening nearly large enough for it to squeeze inside.

The creature lifted its fist to collapse the mouth of the cave. Constable Stoggin braced himself a moment, steadying his nerves. He took a deep breath . . . and shouted at the very top of his lungs.

"HEY!"

The Puncher shuddered and then froze, mouth agape. Its eyes opened wide and turned white, like two great pearls; its arms dropped to its sides. The creature began to sway. It fell with a ground-rumbling crash along the bank of the river. Everyone heard and felt the thunderous clatter from inside. A few ventured a peek from behind the falls. The creature lay by the river, unmoving, surrounded by the boulders it pulled from the mountain. One at a time, the people came out from hiding.

Jat joined Thumbridge in searching the surrounding woods for Constable Stoggin. They found him on his back, body broken, in a patch of moss.

"Are you . . . you did it, sir! You brought it down," said his son.

The constable opened his eyes and then winced in pain. "Startle . . . It's startle . . . that's the one," he said.

"You'll be okay," said Thumbridge, but his face showed he did not believe it.

"Looked . . . into . . . too many . . . giant's ears . . . ," said his father. "Too . . . many . . ."

FIFTEEN

Over

Newton awoke surrounded by three giants and Greyelm, the Puncher who'd knocked him out. He sat up and looked around. Everything looked blurry. The mountain spun in a slow, wobbly circle. He felt behind him. His back was still dangerously close to the edge of the deep ravine. There was nowhere to run.

"*Fi fo*, you hit hard," he said to the Puncher. Greyelm stared at him, its face expressionless.

"You did not turn to stone," said a giant. "Have you found your courage?"

Newton tried to see who was speaking. One eye was swollen shut. The giants in front of him shimmered in and out of view. He knew Crag from his throaty voice, though, and the smell of his blood. To Newton, Crag smelled like mudcheese.

"I control it now, Crag," he said. "Can you?" Although lately, parts of him have been turning and unturning, and he did not know why.

"We traveled far to find you, Broont. We lose giants because of you."

"That was not of my asking." His head was slowly clearing. The ripples of throbbing pain from the Puncher's blows faded between his ears.

Marlite stepped forward. She bent down, face-to-face with her captive.

"You forced us to, Newton. We give our own lives for the giants in our land. We travel the seas for them. You, Newton, you run in fear. You hide your shaking knees across great oceans."

"You called me Newton," said the giant.

"I respect your name choosing. Though it is hard on a giant's tongue. You are smart, Newton. But you care only for Newton."

"Marlite. How did you get here? Why are you here?"

"Your friend Pryat. You told him you were of a plan to float on trees to the Great Sea. He told us."

"'Your' friend Pryat? Is he no longer a friend of Marlite of the holygiants? We three were as friends. As *close* friends, through the passing seasons of our giantling days."

"A holygiant can *have* no friends."

"Pryat would not tell you anything, Marlite. He would not put *this* giant in danger."

"He thought you dead —*Everstone* beneath the sea. He told us of you because it would not matter, he was of a thought."

"Then why didn't you believe him?"

"Because the skyfire still streaks above our land, Broont," said Crag.

Newton turned toward his voice. "As it has since the earliest of days. But no giant has taken to notice it until one landed where we live. Crag. Why are you here? You are Elder Council. You set your *own* boots after this foolish giant?"

"This Elder Council giant is not happy about that, Broont."

"Newton."

"BROONT! The sky still burns with the dragon's anger. We have been of a long time in travel. We do not know what more has been set to flame since we left. Because YOU, Broont, YOU are too great a coward to stand and take in the Makers' Voice!"

Newton turned to the third giant, who had remained silent. He was slightly shorter than the other two and considerably shorter than the Puncher. His bald head was covered in lumps, mapping a lifetime of head poundings by giants he had a knack for angering. "Who are you? This giant is guessing you are not here to be of help to him."

"Aphanfel."

"He found where Pryat was hiding after he freed you," said Marlite.

"This one does a little spying. This one does a little catching. This one does a little adventuring," said Aphanfel, in a dancing voice.

"And that one," said Crag, pointing to the spy, "gets a little *take-take* if he returns with *that* one." He pointed to Newton.

Newton wondered what the take-take would be for the giant who brought him back. To take without a give was a great treasure. A giant could take whatever he wanted, from any giant, without having to make balance.

"You are of an anger toward me because you get nothing when we bring him back."

"Quiet, Aphanfel," snapped Crag. "Elders do not need things they vow to not accept."

"We all know that not to be true for you," said Newton.

"Up, Newton. We are all going back," said Marlite. "I am not sure yet how, but it is what we are doing."

Newton got to his feet. This time the Puncher didn't stop him. He turned and faced the Elder. "Oh, and I *stood* and *heard* the Makers, Crag. This giant will go with you. And this giant will face the Makers again. Then there will be no more Newton. *Fi!* No more *Broont*. But there will also be no more of another thing when we return."

"What?" asked Crag.

"Skyfire!" said Newton. "It is ending. You were not of a need to seek me out."

"You cannot know this," said Crag. "You have been here, cowering in the sand."

"Crag—" Newton gave up. They would not have come this far if they were of a mind that could be changed. He said simply, "If the skyfire still falls, I will take in the Makers' words until I am a pile of ash. The skyfire will fall because the skyfire will fall. I cannot end it. You cannot end it. It will end when it ends, and it is ending now, if it has not already."

Marlite seemed to consider this a moment. "How do you know this?" she asked.

"My eyes, Marlite! My eyes read the truth. I made a thing that shows me the stars. First at home. Then Ooda burned it.

But I made one here, too. Their sky is our sky. If it ends here, it ends at home. And the skyfire, or *shooting stars*, falls less than when this giant arrived."

"The more Broont talks," said Crag, "the more Broont makes trouble, for Broont and all giants. Let this giant ask you a question: Do the Makers' words consume you?"

Newton said nothing.

"Do they?" asked Marlite.

"Why?" asked Newton.

"Because," said Crag. "It proves you are guilty of angering the Makers."

"It proves nothing," said Newton. For a while, he hadn't noticed the pain buzzing in his chest. Crag's words seemed to have awakened it.

"Can we go?" asked Aphanfel.

"How? How do we get back?" asked Newton.

"Our tree stacks float between the Great Sea and the sea of flames," said Crag. "Gossan turned to Everstone to make this so. He sits at the sea bottom with the trees tied to him. Another giant who died for selfish Broont."

"Who else died?" asked Newton.

Aphanfel started counting on his fingers. "Opal turned and sank. Tanzan turned and sank. Kaolin fed a serpent. Pryat . . ."

"PRYAT? What happened to Pryat?"

"His boots rode a different stream," said Crag.

"There were five currents at the spinning waters," said Marlite. "We took the red, because fire we know. And I thought fire *you* know. His tree stack was behind us and got caught in the white ice." The giantess looked away from

Newton. "He is . . . gone. Or he is where the ice current brought him."

Newton glared at the holygiant through his good eye. "You say this as if it does not bring you sadness, Marlite."

"You cannot read what is inside of me . . . BROONT!" she spat.

Newton sniffed in her direction and then smiled sadly. "I can, though."

"Pegma and Gabroc made him go. This giantess thinks it was not much matter to him. He believes he was of a fault in what happened to you."

"Oaf. It was not him. It was you," said Newton.

"We go," she huffed.

The wounded giant staggered forward. He was still unsteady after the bout with Greyelm. The Puncher stiffened, waiting for the smaller giant to try something. But what could he do? *My prying has sent my friend to his icy death*, he thought. *Other giants have died. My mans friends here are in danger. If I had stayed on the Iron Thorn, much would be better for many.* He thought again of Pryat, and a simmering anger grew from the sadness.

"Will Flintoak be back?" Aphanfel asked Crag. "We need food."

"If there is food, he will find it." Flintoak, the other Puncher, had been sent to find food before they left. He was to bring what he scavenged back to where they would reenter the flaming tide.

Newton feared what Flintoak would consider food. Would he have gathered some of his friends? He hoped they'd stayed at the falls. The Puncher would have been able to cover that distance in half the time it took him. And he knew the Apooncha could smell blood from a good distance, even when it still flowed inside a body. *One small mans, maybe not, but many together?*

Newton stopped. "Wait. An oath. You must give oath to leave here without hurting the mans and womans. Let Flintoak collect their ox cows and gooses. But he cannot harm the peoples."

"Peoples?" asked Marlite.

"The mans."

"What is that?" asked Crag.

"This giant can make our journey home one of ease, or one of struggle. Give oath, or it will be one of struggle."

"What are peoples and mans?" asked Crag.

"They are as small giants." Newton held up his hand. "They are of the size of a giant's hand."

"*Huruuum,*" said Aphanfel. "That sounds like a good bite of food." He had not eaten in weeks, and drool trickled from the corners of his mouth.

"They are not food!" said Newton. "They are of two legs. Two legs, no wings. And they are my friends."

"If they fill a giant's stomach, they are food," said Crag. "We must eat before we leave. I am hoping Flintoak waits with a feast of your peoples and mans!"

Newton realized too late the mistake he had made. He should have never mentioned the mans and womans. *I will not let that happen.*

"They have other food. They have ox cows and goats. You will eat those," he said. "Or this giant will not go with you."

Crag nodded toward the Puncher. "Greyelm is of a thought that you will come with us."

Newton looked at the three giants, sizing them up. He could thrump Crag, maybe. But maybe not. Aphanfel, also maybe. Also, maybe not. Marlite would be of good trouble. She was his size, but holygiants were tricky. They could do things with thoughts and words others could not. Then he looked up at Greyelm. He would have no chance against the Puncher. The giant looked behind him. It was his only escape, but the fall would surely kill him, unless . . .

He closed his eyes and thought of his friends, of Jat. Of Fira and Abeleena. Grumpy old Hinson, and Flora, who fed him *boooks*. Mynar Blodge, who made him things. Fearless Constable Stoggin . . . yes, even him. If these giants found they had a taste for mans, they would stay until there were no mans left. A giant's appetite was everlasting. They were always hungry and could never eat too much. One learned to control that hunger at an early age; it was part of growing into a full giant. But when the food was as plentiful as the hunger, there was no reason to stop eating.

Newton had no fear of the giants that surrounded him. He had no fear of the Puncher. They could only cause him pain and death. He already had the pain. Death, he had beaten back before. But a different terror began to creep through him. He thought of his friends thrown down the drooling maws of these giants. They did not deserve this. And there was nothing he could do to stop it! Not while he was a prisoner. Free, he might have a chance.

The giant took a step back. The rocks beneath his feet began to fracture. *Fira, eaten by giants*, he thought. *Jat, eaten by giants* . . . He pictured Crag's teeth crushing his friend's body. Jat's screams of terror! The skin on his arm hardened. *Pryat lost in the Great Sea* . . . These were not tales but real savagery brought upon those he cared for. He took a step back and looked over the edge. It was a long drop—enough to pull the last breath from his body. He wondered what would happen if he jumped. If he knew, if his *body* knew it was a fatal act, would it turn to stone before he hit the bottom? Or had he lived through so much that nothing would turn him again?

This giant can only do the only thing he can do. He felt his back stiffen at the thought. Newton leaned back and fell.

"GRAB HIM!" shouted Marlite. Her ponytail whipped out to snare the falling prisoner.

She was too late. The giant toppled over the edge of the ravine, just another boulder bouncing in a tumbling avalanche.

SIXTEEN

Thunder in the Mountain

I t was dark. Was it night? *Am I dead?* Newton tried to turn his head side to side. He could barely move. His whole body itched. *Oh*, he remembered. *I turned and fell.* Giants' bodies itch ferociously when they turn from stone to flesh. *Must have been knocked out. Head didn't turn to stone fast enough?* The rocks from the side of the ravine had buried him; how deeply, he could not tell. He tried to move his arms and legs, but they were pinned beneath the rubble. If he didn't break free soon, the giants would do it for him. Father had a saying for this: *"The mallet missed your thumb but cracked your knee."*

"Your son cracked his thumb *and* his knee on this one," he murmured. He took a deep breath. Breathing hurt. It nearly always did, since the Iron Thorn, but this felt worse. "And maybe cracked his shortbones, too," he added. It did not matter; nothing mattered but breaking loose. He had to get back to help his friends. The giant balled his fist, focusing all his strength into his one arm, and hammered at the rocks. They didn't budge.

"You WILL move!" he grunted. He hammered at them again and again. They began to give way. The more room he made, the harder he could hit. At last, his fist broke through to the surface. The debris chinkled and thudded as it skidded down from the opening he'd created. His freed arm reached over and pushed a heavy boulder off his chest. He sucked in a deep breath. Breathing was easier. He rolled to his side and pulled his other arm from the pile. A few moments later, he was standing atop the mound of rubble. Straining his neck and back, he looked up to the ledge from which he'd fallen. *Long drop,* he thought.

The other giants were nowhere in sight, but he knew they would be working their way around to come after him. *Time to move your boots . . .*

He rounded a pinnacle of rocks and something caught his arm. It yanked him back, spinning him around and dropping him onto his face. Newton rolled over. Crag stood above him, madly scratching his chest. *He just turned back.*

Crag stopped scratching. He barreled forward and battered Newton's body with his fists and boots. Newton's raised arms deflected many of the blows, but enough were landing to keep him down. He spun on his back and kicked Crag in the knee. The Elder's foot shot out behind him and he crashed down onto his chin. Newton took the opportunity to get to his feet.

"You jumped?" he asked.

Crag stood up, too. "Do not like high places. Knew I would turn before I hit."

"Why do you want me so bad? I am of a thought it is about more than skyfire."

"Sometimes," said Crag, between breaths, "a giant just does not like a giant. Or his Everstone father, or Everstone mother." He ran forward and threw himself at Newton. They both tumbled back down to the ground. Crag got up first. He picked up the other giant and slammed him into the mountain wall. The Elder was twice Newton's age but strong as a moundbull. The ground shuddered and rumbled as the rocks above broke loose and buried both of them. Newton broke free first. He could barely breathe again. The fall had hurt him, but this battle with Crag was burning up the last of his strength.

Crag kicked away the boulders that covered him and climbed slowly to his feet. He stumbled toward his enemy, arms in the air, and pounded on Newton. Newton pounded him back, matching him blow for blow. The valley echoed with the thunderous booming of giants' fists on giants' bodies. This went on and on, neither willing to concede defeat. In time, Newton could barely raise his arms.

"Wait," he said. "Wait . . ." He heard something dripping and looked down. It was the blood pouring from his battered nose. A puddle of blue gathered on the flat rock, spilling over the sides. He had taken a bad beating. Newton tried to close his fingers into a fist. His skin had grown so rigid, they were hard to move. *But I'm not turning.* He looked at Crag. He was banged up, too.

Crag sniffed. "I smell Broont's insides . . . on the out-side . . . His blood smells of fear. And of the sickness of the Makers' Voice. It *does* live inside you! They *did* choose to . . . punish you!"

"No," huffed Newton. "I was speared by lightning atop . . . a tall stick."

"Will you give in to the fear I . . . smell in your dripping blood? Will I be soon pounding a *stone* giant into sand?"

"You will notice . . . this giant . . . has not turned," said Newton. "But wait." He held up his hand. "You need me . . . alive . . . for the Iron . . . Thorn."

"No," said Crag. "We . . . do not. The Makers will thank this giant . . . for sparing their ears . . . from your words."

"I end this fight . . . Newton ends it . . ." said Newton. He dropped his hands and bowed his head.

Crag stepped forward. He reached out to grab the defeated giant's shoulder. Newton launched his fist with everything he had left into the ribs just below Crag's armpit. It struck with a deep crunch, cracking several of the bones. Crag fell back and then stumbled forward onto his knees. His throat gurgled with each breath.

"Broont . . . lies? Broont grinds a . . . a giant's honor . . . into the sand?"

"No," said Newton. He stepped up to Crag and yanked on his ear, a sign of contempt for a giant not worthy to pound. The Elder winced in pain. "Newton spoke true . . . Newton ended this fight." He released Crag's ear and limped off to Blackpoint Falls.

SEVENTEEN

Ring Around the Moon

It was late evening when Newton finally stopped to rest. He knew this would allow the other giants to close the distance between them, but at this point he was falling forward more than running. Even if he kept moving, they would soon overtake him. Crag was hurt, but his legs still worked. *He might have trouble breathing, though, I am of a hope. I do not like breaking another giant's bones. But I do not like more them breaking my own.* Aphanfel, Marlite, and the Puncher would have long since caught up with Crag and would be following his scent. As careful as he was to leave behind as few tracking clues as possible, one could not hide the smell of one's blood from the nose of a healthy giant, whether it ran inside him or out. It lingered in the air long after the giant had passed.

Newton leaned back against a tall tree and slid to the ground. His legs felt like two dead stumps. He wondered if he'd be able to stand on them again. He rapped his thighs with his knuckles and thought they felt almost halfway to stone. The giant stared through the branches, searching the stars. It calmed him, slowed his breaths. So great a place above him, endless giants could walk endless nights and never reach the end of it. It was a forever place.

Here, for a moment, on this tiny land, his problems were as nothing. *No, they are of something. But in a far time to come, something will be as nothing again. Why does my heart reach for the sky after all the trouble it has brought to me? Have you no answers for your friend down here?* The night sky was too bright to see much of what it held, the full moon dimming the stars. He turned his focus to the glowing orb, avoiding looking at it directly, as it would make seeing in the dark more difficult. Then he saw the ring. It circled the moon in a frosty haze. *The ring around the moon.* The giant had seen this before, but it was Jat who had taught him what it meant. Just a winter ago he and the boy sat beneath a ringed moon on the shore of the Fire Sea:

"I don't know how, or why, but that circle around the moon means a storm's coming," Jat said.

"I have seen this through my farlooker back home," said Newton. *"The ring is not around the moon. It is the light of the moon shining through haze high in the sky."*

"Whatever makes it happen, rain's coming soon," said the boy.

And he was right. It poured the next day.

Giants cannot smell giants in the heavy rain, thought Newton, back on the mountain. *I am of a thought I can use this.* Water, he knew, drowns a giant's blood odor. It could hide where he was going. The problem was, the plan growing in his head would place him right in the hands of his pursuers if the rain did not come at the right time—or if it came and was not enough. *Or if it doesn't come at all* . . . While he knew they would catch him if he simply kept running, he didn't want to just give himself up to them. He looked up at the moon, encircled by the glowing ring. It looked like a great eye, staring back at him. His finger scratched out the shapes in the dirt between his feet.

"What is in the sky is now at Newton's feet. This giant hopes it will stay with him and keep him safe." He stared down, smiling dreamily at circles. Suddenly the Makers' Voice exploded inside him. He had held it back for days, but the pain slipped past his guard and pulled him down into a ball. It was so great, it turned him to stone.

Newton awoke, his body itching madly. The pain from the Voice was back to a low murmuring crackle. *This makes me turn now? That is NOT of a good thing!* What if he'd turned at the wrong time? *How long did it last?* The giant stood up. His arms and legs were growing more stiff, his skin more hard. *Cannot be of worry now,* he thought. He walked to a clearing and looked out at the bright red sky on the horizon. The sun had not yet risen, but the moon moved on. It was very early morning. Wispy streaks of clouds crawled high above. The giant sniffed. He was still alone.

He had no idea when the rain would actually start, or if it would come at all, but this was his last and only chance. He barreled through the woods, knocking over trees, rolling boulders, and scraping deep furrows in the trail as he went along. Newton wanted to be sure Crag and the others went this way even after they could no longer smell him. This would take them down the other side of the mountain, away from Blackpoint Falls. While his plan would delay his own return to the mans and womans, it should lead the giants far away from them. *And*, he thought, *it could save this giant's own grubbly hide.*

The red morning sky slowly muddied into a smoky blue. Heavy, murky clouds slid across the valley. *Time to stop.* He turned around and retraced his steps. Newton had scratched images of the ringed moon onto boulders along the way. He knew the giants would not know their meaning but hoped the mystery of it would make them pause, maybe even frighten them some, if just for a moment.

The sky had grown dark in the time it took to make it back to the head of his false trail. Clouds the color of wet ash swirled low overhead. A strong breeze stirred the tops of the trees. A storm was coming. *But when?* He took the time to make extra sure they would not miss where he wanted them to go. The plan was to stay just ahead of them until the rain came down, and then cut uphill, off the false trail, as soon as they could no longer smell him. He'd be extra careful not to leave behind any visual clues of his new route. Then he would skirt the side of the mountain to make his way to the falls.

"Broont . . . oont . . . oont . . . ! We come for you . . . ou . . . ou . . . !" echoed a voice in the valley. "We know you are close . . . ose . . . ose . . ."

Aphanfel. Newton looked up. Still no rain. This was not going to work, and now he had lost a whole morning he could have spent escaping. He looked up the mountain.

Trees moved in the distance. Greyelm's head floated above the canopy.

"Broont . . . oont . . . oont . . . ! We come . . . ome . . . ! We come to break . . . eak your bones . . . ones . . . ones . . . ! We come to make . . . ake you stones . . . ones . . . ones . . . !"

Newton paced in circles at the trailhead. *Do I run? Do I let them get more close?* He didn't want to turn off the false trail from its end. It would take away his head start. The sooner he could get himself going in the right direction, the more ground he could put between them—*if* they kept going in the wrong direction when the trail ended. *If* it were raining. *If . . . if. IF! It is not raining!* Without the storm, he was finished either way. He picked up a rock and threw it up at the clouds, hoping to poke a hole in it.

"Let your water out!" he shouted.

He would wait, but not much longer. Newton could see the Puncher. Whether or not it saw him, he didn't know. The giant sniffed and picked up a faint, pungent odor. *Haroomph . . . if this giant can smell that giant, that giant can smell this giant . . .* He turned back toward his trap. Without the rain, he was back to trying to outrun them. *I will have to go this way,* he thought. *They cannot know where this giant truly wishes to go.* Newton took a deep breath and began to run down the trail. Then he stopped. *No . . . No . . .*

"NO!" he rumbled. "NO! No more running!" *Father would not run. Mother would not run. Ooda would not run. PRYAT WOULD RUN—RIGHT AT THEM! This giant will stand. This giant will fight.*

Then Newton felt it burst into his body for the first time in his life. Other giants felt it often—*Pryat very.* He usually

· 153 ·

made a point to steer clear of them when they did. The *squall*, it was called, the kill-or-die madness to which giants find themselves prone. It is as much part of them as their arms and legs. It is what makes giants what they are. It is what nearly thrumped them into bones and dust countless times in history.

It did not matter that he was outnumbered. If he was going to be captured, it wouldn't be as some frightened moor-hare. He was tired, bloody, and beaten. It did not matter. Pain scorched his insides. It did not matter. He was a giant and he would die as a giant, and maybe take some with him. He wrapped his arms around a tree and tore it from the ground. Newton heaved it over his head and waited. If not for the madness, he'd be surprised he was smiling.

Greyelm was the first to come. The Puncher tromped through the trees, making no effort to go around them. In a few short moments, it was upon him.

Newton heard it, pattering on the leaves. Then he felt it. Raindrops. The clouds tore open, dropping a torrent of rain on the mountainside. Rivulets of water surged around the giant's feet. *Haroomph*, thought Newton, pushing back the madness. *Maybe this is* not *the time to fight?*

Greyelm charged at him. Newton hurled the tree at it, knocking it to the wet ground. The Puncher landed on its back. It struggled to rise on the slippery, moss-covered rocks. Newton turned and ran down the trail. He looked back and saw Aphanfel help up the fallen giant. The rain was falling so hard, he could barely see where he was going, but he had made his trail easy to follow. They would be right behind him. Newton sniffed. He could smell nothing but the dizzy-ingly sweet, scent-masking downpour. He stepped off the trail and ducked behind a pile of boulders. The squall inside him was gone, almost as quickly as it came. It would not be of help to him, so he let it go. He had heard that could not be done. But he had heard a lot of things that were not of truth and yet said to be so.

Greyelm splashed past him, followed by Aphanfel. And then, limping along, came Crag. None saw or smelled him.

Where is Marlite? wondered Newton. He waited a bit longer. When she failed to show, he turned and picked his way, as gingerly as a giant's boots could take him, up the mountain.

EIGHTEEN

An Unexpected Friend

T he villagers gathered around the fallen Puncher.

"Is it dead?" someone asked.

Bonnie Mullein had run back to the falls after the Puncher marched past her. The girl squeezed through the crowd, who seemed eager for a look, but from a safe distance. She cautiously approached its head.

"Maybe you are close enough?" warned Bill Mullein, her father. Bonnie ignored him, as she usually did.

She picked up a stick and poked the Puncher, snapping the stick. Flintoak had not moved since collapsing. Its eyes remained open but appeared frozen in their deep sockets like balls of ice.

"I don't know," she said. "Doesn't look like it's breathing."

"*Do* they even breathe?" asked Lord Ellery.

"I don't know that, either," said Bonnie. "It didn't turn to stone, though."

"They breathe," said Lady Ellery. "But this one has breathed its last."

"What befell this creature?" The lord turned to Jat. "I thought you said a scare *enstoneates* them."

"I just told you what Newton told me once. It didn't turn it to stone, but it did stop it."

Suddenly, the Puncher's mouth moved. They all jumped back.

Lord Ellery shrieked, "It lives yet!"

The lips opened, and out squeezed a stout young man. He was covered head to toe in brown slime and chunks of animal parts.

"Budge!" shouted Bonnie. She ran up and embraced her fellow deputy. "Ugh, you're disgusting!"

"Apparently they don't chew their food," he said.

"What was it like in there?" asked Allander Quint. "The other person . . . Did you see . . . were you alone in . . . ?"

"You do not want to know, Lander," said Budge. Jat walked up to him and shook his hand.

"I can't believe you pulled us out of the way of this thing. You saved our lives, Budge. Thank you!"

The deputy shrugged. "Tell my dad that. Maybe now he'll let me quit."

Elspeth Bowrider, the village healer, returned from attending Constable Stoggin.

"How is he?" asked Lady Ellery.

She shook her head sadly. "Thumbridge is with him. He lost a father today. We lost a very good man." The group went silent.

"Now what?" asked Bonnie, wiping a tear from her eye. "Should I go back to my post? There might be more of them coming."

"I think so," said Jat. "I'll go with you. I want to go back to the village. I think they will come through there first if they decide to head here, which I think they will. This thing left a path an ocean wide."

"I want you to stay here," said Fira, throwing a disapproving look at Bonnie. The girl shrugged, and Fira turned back to her son. "There's nothing you can do back home." Jat started to protest but was stopped by his mother's glare. He looked over to Bonnie, who nodded in agreement.

"Are we even safe *here* anymore?" asked Fenton Quigley. He couldn't take his eyes off the giant.

"If this one couldn't reach us, then perchance the others, too, may find themselves unable," said Lady Ellery.

Flora walked up for a closer look at the Puncher. "*Our giant was able to fit in the cavern," said Flora. "Who's to say the other ones cannot?" No one had an answer.

"Yeah, that, and the entrance is a lot bigger now," said Bonnie. "If the constable didn't stop this thing . . ."

"I wasn't made for this," said Lord Ellery. "This is a far skippy-step from settling boundary disputes or . . . who owes whom coppers, or . . . or flower worms."

"We never thought you were much good at those things, either," said Flora. Lord Ellery sniffed and turned away.

"Our giant said we should wait here. I think we should," she added.

"What if you and I were to return home," said the lord to his wife. "There is no good reason for us to be here."

"Don't you dare say that a second time!" scolded Lady Ellery. "We shall do this together. And we are all staying right here!"

"Then that is what shall be done, then," snipped Ellery.

It was decided that with the runners keeping watch along the trail, they all didn't have to wait crammed into the cavern. Though some chose to do so. A few families decided to take their chances away from the rest, reasoning, perhaps correctly, that being part of a crowd would make them easier to find.

Constable Stoggin was carried inside the cave. He would be buried back in town when it was safe to return. He'd spent his entire life there and died carrying out the charge he had proudly accepted: to protect the people.

The next morning, Jat left the cavern for some fresh air. Suddenly, he was shoved from behind. He landed on his face, splitting his lip. The boy rolled over to see Durd standing above him.

"You're alive!" said Jat.

"Not because of you, Sootyboy. It was your monster friends that did this to us. They crushed our home. My brother . . ."

"They're not my friends, Durd, and you know it. And I don't know if you noticed, but I'm not sooty anymore. You're looking more filthy than I am, or anyone here," said Jat, standing up. "I'm not going to take this from you. Especially not now!"

"Neither am I," said Mason Twirp, stepping up beside him.

Little Ran, who was not much bigger than Abeleena, was at his side. "Three to one," he said.

"Pshh . . . I can take both of you. Little Ran, you don't even count." Durd picked up a heavy stick. He walked up to Jat and pressed his face into his. "You still stink," he said. He pulled away and shoved him again, knocking him onto his back. Jat jumped up and was about to plow into the other boy, when he saw someone he recognized in the distance.

"Uh-oh," he said.

"HEY! DURD!" came a shout.

Durd turned around. "Sack! You're alive?"

Sack ran up to his brother and punched his shoulder. "You're alive, too? Ma?"

"Yeah, we were out back when that thing crushed our house. Thought you were inside! Then we took the back trails to here. Got here this morning." Durd turned and faced the other three. "Two to TWO," he said with a grin. "You still don't count, Little Ran. Did you want to find any more friends for us to knock around? To make it even? I was going to do it because I was mad, but now I'm happy, so it'll be more fun." He wound up, ready to swing the stick. Sack leapt forward and tackled his brother. "What are you doing, Sack?"

Sack got up and ran at Jat. He wrapped his arms around him and lifted him up in the air. Sack was nearly twice his weight and squeezed the breath out of the boy. He set him back on the ground.

"You saved my life against that thing," he said. "I owe you. I owe you a lot!"

"Erm . . . you're welcome?"

Durd got to his feet. "Dirty Sootyboy saved your life? What are you talking about?"

Sack spun around to his brother and poked him in the chest with his finger. "You call him that again, and I'll knock your head off." He grabbed his brother by the collar and led him back to go look for his ma.

The three boys stood there, wide-eyed, in silence. In the distance they heard, "Sootyboy saved your . . . ? OOF! Sorry, okay! Okay!"

Two days passed. Jat, Fira, and Abeleena sat against the outer wall of the cavern, sharing a heel of bread. Like most of the villagers, they wanted to stay within quick running distance to the entrance behind the falls. It had rained hard the day before and the falls roared and churned with the extra volume of water. There was no going in or out without getting soaked.

"I keep thinking of how brave you were, Jat, riding that thing here the other day," said his mother. "It's hard to think of your son in that kind of danger. I keep trying not to, but then my heart swells with pride. And then that turns to anger. Aagh! You shouldn't do these things! Just be a normal kid!"

Jat took in a deep breath and let it out. He looked down at his torn-off nails. "I'm not brave. If only you knew how scared I was," he said. "I didn't even know you could be that scared!"

"But that's what makes a person brave; doing things they have to do even when they're scared. You've always been like that. It's why my hair turns gray."

"Mother . . . I'm thinking of leaving soon—if we make it through this."

"I know. It's been coming. That big, dumb giant filled your head with adventures. But your father left his mother once. I left mine. It is how it is."

"That's exactly what the 'big, dumb giant' said. You're not mad?"

Fira smiled, though there was a sadness behind it. "Mad? No. Sad? Yes. You are a good son, Jat. A good . . . man. Your father would be so proud of you. You took care of your family. You gave up being a kid because you had to. But this village is too small for you. I know you need to find your own life. And when you do, you will come home—often!—and tell me about it. You'll share it with your old mother."

Jat's eyes were welling with tears. He looked away so she wouldn't see them. "I will, Mother." He ran his sleeve across his face. "Still, it's hard to imagine actually setting out. I think of it and get excited. I picture myself in places, having adventures, seeing things that I don't even know exist. Then . . . I think of not seeing you, and I don't know if I can do it. It's easy to think these things. It's hard to actually do them."

"Okay, don't leave, then," said his mother, bumping him playfully with her shoulder. "It's settled."

"I . . . you'll still have Abeleena."

Fira gave her daughter a squeeze. "For now, at least. And, for now, I still have both of you."

"Newton!" said Abeleena.

"Well, no," said Fira. "I won't *have* Newton. He is his own man . . . giant."

Abeleena pointed to the trees in the distance. "Mama! Newton!"

Jat jumped to his feet. Newton's head crested the treetops across the valley. He was moving very fast.

"Newton is coming!" shouted the boy.

A roar of excitement rose from the townspeople. They crowded in for a better view by the edge of the river. The giant stumbled through the trees and was soon standing among his friends. He looked far worse for wear than when they'd last seen him. The parts of his face not caked in blood were covered with cuts, mud, leaves, and bruises. The hand he'd used to punch through the rubble was nearly twice its already-enormous size. He held it cradled to his chest. One eye was swollen shut. As soon as he saw the Puncher, he rushed toward it, fists raised in the air. He soon saw that it held no threat.

"I am of a thought you killed it," he said. "I did not think it to be a possible thing. How?"

"Constable Stoggin," said Lady Ellery, and she filled the giant in on what had happened.

"He was the big one in this village—this land-world," said Newton sadly. "I stand small next to him."

"Where are the other giants?" asked Jat.

"They come," said Newton. "I tried to lead them away but only slowed them down. I will keep them after me. You must stay here. Hide in the big cave. I will let them see me and make them chase. It is almost over."

"And when they catch you?" asked Jat. "Why do I have to

keep asking you that? I'm so tired of it! You should care as much about that as I do!"

"They will come close, but they will not catch me. And they are of too much a mind to grab this giant to notice you. And . . ." Newton hesitated. *Should I tell them?* "They are hungry to . . . eat mans and womans. It is my regret and blame . . . They know about you now."

"They would have figured out that someone lived in those houses they crushed," said Flora.

"Oh no! They crushed your houses? *Pound their bones*, this must end! But I will lead them away to my home by the Fire Sea."

"Um . . . what about this?" asked Lord Ellery, pointing to the dead Puncher.

"*Harooomph* . . . That is a problem," said the giant. He could not leave Flintoak here. The other giants would be curious about what had happened to him and might stick around long enough to sniff out the humans. "I will drag him away. This is a big one, though. More and more am I wishing I was a bigger giant."

"I do not think you will be returning," said Lady Ellery.

"I do not think I will," said Newton. "I feel that I am of a need to speak with you more, Lady Ellery."

"Perhaps you may at another time, good giant. Be of strong heart. It has brought you this far."

"None of this was your fault," said Fira. "You are a kind . . . giant. I truly wish you peace in your life. You have earned it."

"Thank you, Fira. Thank you all for your friendship. I wish you were not punished for it. Abeleena, give your mother many smiles. She will return them to you." The little girl hugged his finger. Then Newton saw Flora. She stood in silence, with that same unreadable face, her arms hugging her body. The giant pointed to her, and then to his heart, and then to the sky. He smiled at his teacher. She nodded and smiled back. Newton straightened up slowly.

"What's wrong?" asked Jat.

"What do you mean?"

"You're moving funny. Slow and shaky."

"Stiff," said the giant. "It has been a busy few days, Jat."

"Let's go," said the boy.

"No. You will stay."

"He's right, Jat," said his mother.

"Mother, I brought him to us, and I'm going to see him off. It's important. I am going with him."

"No, you're . . ." Fira closed her eyes and sighed through clenched teeth. Then she stepped forward and embraced her son. "Promise you will come back," she whispered.

"I promise."

"Jat," began Newton.

"I'm not staying. Let's go. And let's go now! We have a Puncher to load."

"Load?"

"Do you want to drag that thing, or . . ." Jat pointed to the two large wagons Newton had used to carry some of the people here. The giant let out a sigh of relief that nearly blew the boy off his feet.

NINETEEN

A Few Happy Memories

Newton pulled the dead Puncher down the long trail that led back to the village. Bonnie and Jat rode on the edge of one of the wagons, feet hanging over the side. Neither wanted to be sitting that close to the creature, but it was the only way they could keep up with Newton. Bonnie was going to replace the boy watching her post along the trail. If the giants changed course and headed up through the village, she wanted someone fast, namely herself, to warn the people.

"You got another fat lip," she said to Jat.

"I know."

"I know how it happened. I also know how you saved his brother's life."

"Who told you?"

"Durd. He said he wants to shake your hand, but he didn't think you would."

"He's right," said Jat.

"So you're kind of a hero now, huh. You fight with bullies. You save lives. You ride giant tree things—I saw you. I couldn't believe it! Who are you, Jat? When did this happen?"

Jat looked at Bonnie, who was smiling broadly. "You're making fun of me, I know it."

"No, Jat, I'm not! Your hair is clean. Your face is . . . I can see it now . . ." She sniffed. "You don't smell like a fireplace anymore. You impress me."

Jat turned red. "Why were you always nice to me? I mean before, when everyone pretty much stayed away?"

"I don't know. I'm just nice. I'm nice to everyone."

Jat laughed. "Oh no, you're not!"

"Well, is that a nice thing to say?"

"Yeah, well . . ."

"I'm jumping off here," said the girl.

"Newton, stop," Jat shouted up to the giant. Newton waited while she climbed down.

"You be careful, Bonnie," said the boy.

"No, *you* be careful! You should have stayed back with the others. What good do you think you can do against giant monsters?"

"Newton needs me. He's in this alone, and I don't want him to be. A man stands with his friends, Bonnie."

Bonnie laughed. "If we all survive this, the next barn dance? I'm saving the first dance for . . ." She poked him in his chest. "You."

Jat blushed again. "You better save *all* the dances for me."

"Whoa! Bold man now that he's a hero. You stay safe, Jat. I mean it!"

"I will. You too."

Newton got them moving again. For a while he said nothing as Jat looked back, watching Bonnie fade into the distance.

"My friend can ride a Puncher's ankle, but is of a fear to embrace a girl-womans," he finally said.

"Shut up," said Jat.

They passed through the deserted village, much of it unrecognizable. Flintoak had done a thorough job tearing it apart. It would take years to rebuild. *There was no need for this*, thought Newton sadly. *Why?* The occasional goat or chicken wandered skittishly through the empty dirt lanes, the few stray animals that had escaped the Puncher's notice. Ned Donnerly's rooster still sat on the weathervane where the bird always sat, despite the fact that the house it was attached to was on its side.

"Should we leave this thing here?" asked Jat. He hopped down from the wagon.

"We could," said Newton. "It is far enough from the falls. I go back to my home now. I need to gather my things."

"For what?"

"I am leaving, Jat."

"I know. But to where? Are we going to hide in the mountains?"

"No. They would just keep looking for me. They would find more mans and more womans and . . . you know. It would not be good. I am going back to the Great Sea. I will make sure they know I escape. They must leave here—your land—and chase me home." Newton sighed. "The giants chase. Newton runs. And so it goes."

"How? You can't bring a raft. It would burn in the Fire Sea before you got there."

"The giants left their floating trees at the edge of the sea. One waits for me now, to bring me back."

"Okay, then how will I go? I can't cross the Fire Sea."

"No, my friend Jat cannot come with me this time. I go to find my other friend, Pryat. He went the way of the ice stream. I must find him before . . ."

"Before what?"

Newton touched his belly. "There is a . . . poison in this giant . . . since the Iron Thorn. You know this. It eats and eats. Soon there will be nothing for it to feed on. It has begun to turn me to stone, I am of a thought."

Jat hollered and began pounding and kicking the dead Puncher's hand. Newton stood silently, watching. The boy kept at it until he exhausted himself. He slid down to the ground, out of breath.

"There has to be a way for me to come with you," he said. "You will need my help. You always do. I teach you things."

"You do. What you taught your friend about the ring around the moon saved his life."

"Yeeeah . . . I wasn't going to say this, because it worked, but you should know that it's not always true. Sometimes it means rain is coming, but that could be in a day or two. Sometimes it doesn't come at all. You were just lucky—we all were."

"If I had known this, I do not know what else I would have done. Maybe not knowing a thing can make one act as if he does. And maybe, on certain times, that is enough."

"Maybe. Newton, there has to be a way I can come with you. We have to find a way to cure you. There is a way, but we just don't know it yet."

"I have thought on this, but my head is an empty bowl of

· 169 ·

answers," said the giant. "And do you not remember what you promised Fira, your mother? That you would return?"

"I will, but I did not say when," said the boy.

"Tricks with tricky words . . . Come with me to my home. We will say goodbye there."

Jat sat a while longer, stubbornly. Then he stood and followed the giant in silence the entire way to the shores of the Fire Sea. The orange tide lapped and crackled at the coal-lined shore. Spilling out from the tide's edge was an endless swath of pale yellow sand. Newton's house could be seen in the far distance, growing from the steep cliffs that lined the edges of the coast. A bit farther off was the great furnace they had built. *I was happy here.*

"You can live here, Jat. It would please this giant if you made this your home." Jat said nothing.

"My friend Jat can make waterstone . . . *glassss* . . . for his people." The giant waited for a response but got none. They kept walking.

They reached Newton's home and went inside. The place was open and airy, but piled high along the walls were books and parts for building improved farlookers. He had almost completed one designed to be carried to a different place. He was of a thought that he could get a better view up in the mountains, away from the light of the Fire Sea. The giant was never satisfied with how the previous teleoscopes worked and continually disassembled and rebuilt them. The walls of his home were cluttered with long strips of smooth white bark covered with writings and drawings he'd made. Sometimes it was easier to figure out problems when there was something to look at. Newton lingered on them a while.

"Come outside," he said. Jat followed him, his moping body dragging unwilling feet.

Newton stood in front of his talking wall. It began by the entrance of the cave, where his home now stood, and stretched beyond what the eye could see. "The story of Newton, a giant in a faraway land," he said. "In time, the rain will wash my silent stories from the cliffs. But that does not bring a sad thought. All begins. All ends." Jat stared down at the sand.

"Look, Jat. Here the giant meets his friend at the firetide. Look how frightened the giant's friend looks." Newton looked at the boy, whose face had been wearing the same scowl since they left the village.

"And here is where the giant made a mountain of snow for his friends. See them sliding down on their wooden planks? Oh, and who is this one?" The giant squinted at the picture. "Yes. It is wild Bonnie. Put down that spear, wild Bonnie, before you prick this giant's toe!" Jat looked up at the picture.

"I am glad that made my friend smile," said Newton. "*I would smile if you would finish my story. You will have to add the Stoggin and the Puncher. And a moon with a ring around it. It did save this giant's life, Jat. You saved his life.*"

"How can I finish your story here, when I am going with you?" asked Jat.

"I do not know how you will cross this," said Newton, pointing to the Fire Sea.

"I haven't figured it out yet, but I will," said the boy. "And you're moving funny. You're going to need my help finding a way to help you."

"Just stiff," said the giant.

"*Or turning to stone,*" the boy muttered.

Newton went back into his home, quickly gathering various lenses, books, and writing tools. He stuffed them all in pockets of his jacket.

"They'll just burn, you know," said Jat.

"No. A giant's clothes do not burn. They will be kept safe."

Jat's face lit up. "What if . . . ?"

"No," said Newton. "You would not be able to breathe beneath the fire. It is many giants deep. It is many bootsteps from the fire to the hot water, and then to the cold water. And then . . ."

Jat slumped down in the chair Newton had made for him.

"Okay. You're right. This is another one of those things where there is no good choice. There just isn't, and I hate this. I hate what's going to happen. It's not right. You didn't do anything wrong, and I hate that you can't make them see it! It's not . . . I just wish . . . UGH!" he said in frustration. He stared angrily at the floor and then sighed. "When are you going?"

Newton looked out the window. It was almost night. The golden palette of the setting sun slowly melted into the glow of the Fire Sea. *This giant will miss seeing this . . .*

"When they come for me," he said. "It will be soon. It is time for you to leave, Jat. They will smell your blood."

"Won't they just grab you and keep you from going after your friend?"

"If they catch me, yes. I will wait to see them come. Then I will run to the sea and let them see me. They will all follow."

"Or one will grab you now and take you home," said a voice from behind.

Newton and Jat turned to the door. A giant blocked the opening.

TWENTY

Chasing Bonnie

Aphanfel came around the scree-covered slope and found Crag sitting against a ledge. The Elder was holding his side.

"Where is Broont?" he asked.

Crag looked up. "He ran."

"You did not stop him?"

"I tried. He . . . tricked me. I think he broke my short-bones." He struggled to his feet.

"Broont thrumped YOU?"

"Quiet, Aphanfel. Or I will thrump *you*. Where is Marlite?"

"The holygiant went a different way. Said she follows minds, not bodies. I am not knowing what that means, but I am of a relief she is not with us. Her smell of magic does not bring comfort to this giant."

"It is not supposed to."

Greyelm tromped around the corner, joining the other two giants. It studied Crag, as if piecing together what had happened. Crag straightened up, trying to lessen the appearance of the beating he'd taken.

"He got thrumped by Broont," said Aphanfel with a grin.

Crag swung at the young spy. Aphanfel stepped back and the blow grazed his shoulder. He returned the punch, connecting with Crag's broken ribs. The injured giant let loose a muted, bubbly scream.

Suddenly, Greyelm spun away from Aphanfel and whipped back again, launching its fist squarely on the spy's chest. Aphanfel crashed through a stack of boulders and continued through the air until coming to a stop at the edge of the valley. Crag limped over to him, followed by the stoic Puncher.

"I told you 'quiet,'" he said. "You serve the Council. I am the Council here. Greyelm serves me, too, as your body now tells you."

Aphanfel struggled to his feet. "This giant meant no insult," he wheezed.

"Good," said Crag. "We go now after that sneaking coward."

The three giants followed Newton's path. Newton had a small lead on them, and he likely knew where he was going. Greyelm, whose longer legs carried him faster, led the way. Crag limped along behind them. He was hurting from his battle with the runaway giant. The giant would heal, but that would take time. After a day of chasing, he had them stop for the night.

"Broont will be stopping, too," he said. "He can barely walk."

"Or you can barely walk," said Aphanfel. Crag ignored that one.

They continued the chase the next morning under the darkening sky. Just as they were about to catch up to Newton, the giant ambushed the Puncher and ran down the mountain. Rain exploded from the clouds as the three took off after him.

"I cannot smell him," shouted Aphanfel.

"It is of no matter," said Crag. "His boots tell us where he goes." They came to one of Newton's drawings on a rock.

"See? Only Broont would do this," said Crag.

"What is it?" asked the spy, his eyes wide with fear.

Crag looked at the circle drawn around a circle. Then he looked up at Aphanfel. "It looks like your eye," he said.

"Does Broont watch us with these rocks?"

"No," said the Elder, "but this giant believes it is what Broont wants us to think."

"I do not like it at all," said Aphanfel. "It smells of holy-giant magic."

"We talk, he runs. That is his magic."

The rain began to ease. The giants had nearly reached the end of Newton's false trail when Aphanfel called for them to stop.

"This is not right," he said. "There are no bootprints. If he was in front of us, we would see bootprints in the mud." He tested the air with his nose. "And we should smell his blood now that the rain is stopping. He went off this trail."

They turned around. In time, Aphanfel found Newton's side trail up the mountain. "He went up this way," he shouted.

They traveled a full day without stopping and reached the falls before sunset.

"*Fi fo*, I smell the blood of *something* here," said Aphanfel. "I do not know what it is."

Crag sniffed. "It is many of the same thing," he said. "They are not animals. And I smell . . . Flintoak? But where is he?"

A wail exploded from Greyelm. It ran to where its partner had fallen and sniffed the ground. It picked up a scale of thick skin and brought it up to its dull black eyes. The Puncher arched back and let loose another bloodcurdling cry. It stood and looked around, its normally expressionless face twisted in barbarous rage.

"They can make noise?" asked Aphanfel quietly. "Flintoak? Did something happen to him?"

"That is of my thought," said Crag. "They are brothers. There is something here. It did something to Flintoak. Or *they* did something."

"How can anything hurt the Apooncha?" asked the spy. "And where is his body? Did Broont do this?"

"I am not of that knowledge, Aphanfel. Look." He pointed to the trail left behind by Newton. "Whatever did this went through there. Greyelm! This way!"

Bonnie Mullein hid behind a thick, low-branched cedar along the path. She had been sitting quietly just moments before, with little to do but wait for something to happen. It would be dark soon. The darkness would help keep her hidden. "But can they smell me?" she asked herself. She gave her shirt a sniff. "Uh-oh."

Greyelm's wailing back at the falls literally shook her to

her core. She pushed deeper into the branches of the tree. The ground began to shake. The pounding footsteps of the approaching giants forced all bearers of feather, fur, and hoof to flee their advance. She peeked out from the needles. Trees parted in the distance. They would be going right by her, and very soon.

Little time had passed since Jat and Newton had dropped her off.

"They need more time," she whispered to herself. "They'll catch them . . ." She grabbed her hair and pulled, squeezing her eyes shut. "What-to-do-what-to-do-what-to-do . . . ?"

The giants came barreling down the path. The bald one up front was the same size as Newton, about the height of the surrounding trees. He had a narrow, weasely face with close-set, darting gray eyes. He was followed by a taller, plumper giant with a wiry beard caked in what appeared to be blood—but it was *blue*. Behind him was another Puncher, nearly identical to the one dropped at the falls.

"Jat, if you can do this, I can," she whispered. "Agh! Am I going to do this? I can't believe I'm going to do this." She pulled her leather gloves from her pocket and slid them over her hands. The first giant clomped past her. "I'm not going to do this," she said under her breath. She yanked her boots tight above her calves. The second one followed. "No. I'm not doing this." As soon as the Puncher passed the cedar tree, she scurried out and ran after it. "I'm doing this!" Its foot struck the ground and she leapt onto the back of its ankle and held on. The Puncher felt nothing and continued, jarring the bones of the girl's body with each step.

They quickly arrived at the village. The three giants

stopped. Flintoak's body spilled over two large wagons in the center of town. Greyelm let out another chilling wail. Bonnie dropped off its ankle and ducked behind an overturned water trough. She watched the tree creature inspect its fallen companion. The other two giants stood back away from it. Neither seemed eager to get too close to the grieving Puncher.

Suddenly, Greyelm turned away from Flintoak. It stared at the path its brother had made from the shores of the Fire Sea. The Puncher let out an explosive huff and marched toward it. The other two giants looked at each other and followed.

"No," Bonnie whispered to herself. "They're too close behind!" She stood up from behind the trough and shouted, "HERE! I'M HERE!" Her voice crackled in fear, but they must have heard her because two of them stopped.

"HERE I AM! COME GET ME, STUPID . . . OAFS!"

"Greyelm, wait!" shouted Crag. The Puncher stopped. "We have one."

In just three steps, the giants were standing above the girl.

"It's Newton!" she screamed, pointing behind them. They turned as one, expecting the fugitive giant to jump them. But there was no Newton. Bonnie darted into the nearest building. The Puncher stepped forward and with a single swipe, swept it off its foundation. The girl had already left through the back window a split second before it was no more. She barely made it to the next building. That, too, was swept away by the Puncher. The giants huddled over the wreckage.

"I smell her blood, but I do not see her," said Aphanfel. He scraped away what was left of the building. She wasn't there.

"She is among the timbers," said Crag. They turned and

began rolling over the walls and roof lying in a nearby heap. Bonnie stuck her head up from the root cellar. She quietly crawled out and hurried to the barn at the end of the dusty street, hugging the sides of the buildings and debris from the first Puncher's visit. She peeked inside. It was filled with geese. Bonnie quietly cracked open the door. "Go. Go," she whispered. "You're not safe here!" The geese stayed put. She went around to the back, where the horses normally grazed. They were gone. She grabbed her hair again.

"What-to-do-what-to-do-what-to-do?" Then, at the far end of the field, she saw a lone horse.

"Trapper!" she nearly shouted, and then quickly covered her mouth. They didn't hear her over the sound of the flock of geese exploding noisily from the barn. She ran across the grass, checking behind her for giants. Two of them were trying, with little success, to catch the frantic birds. The big, tree-like monster remained focused on finding her, knocking over the few buildings left standing. In an odd twist of luck for Ned Donnerly, his barn was turned right side up. Although Aphanfel ate the rooster.

Bonnie approached the horse, which was noticeably frightened.

"Easy, girl . . . You remember me, yes?" She pulled her glove off and held out her hand. The horse nuzzled her palm. "Okay, are you still as fast as you used to be?"

Bonnie had no time to find a saddle or reins. She had ridden bareback before, but at just a light trot.

"Please don't shake me loose," she said as she climbed onto the horse and rode off toward the woods. There was a horseshoe trail at the edge that circled around for about ten miles before leading back to the village. She had traveled it many times.

"Let's see how much of their time we can waste," she said to the horse. "Are you up for this? Because I really hope you are!" She stopped at the edge of the trail. The sun was dropping below the treetops, throwing long shadows across the field.

"OVER HERE, YOU DUMB COWS!"

The giants stopped and turned toward the girl on the horse. They pounded after her.

"Uh-oh, they are fast," said Bonnie. She spurred the horse forward and galloped down the path.

TWENTY-ONE

Three Giantlings

"A greeting, Marlite," said Newton.

"A greeting, Newton," said the holygiant. "Were you not going to wait for us?"

Marlite was about Newton's size, slightly less bulky, and with a nose slightly more bulbous. Around her head was the band of silver worn by all holygiants. A braided lock of rusty-orange hair ran down her back and trailed behind her on the ground. Sometimes it moved on its own, like a writhing snake. Holygiants had ways about them that other giants found unsettling. This particular one was Marlite's. Her red robes were tattered from her long journey across the sea, followed by an unending chase through the mountains and forest in pursuit of a runaway giant. She did not look angry, though. In fact, she looked somewhat relieved. Newton stared into her dark eyes, searching for the familiar friend he'd once played with as a young giant.

"Get behind me, Jat." The boy did as he was told.

"Let him go," he said to the holygiant.

"It can go," said Marlite. "It is only you we want."

Newton tried to look behind her. "We? Where are the others?"

"They come soon." She looked past his shoulder at the ladder through the ceiling. "Where does this go?" she asked.

Newton smiled. "I will show you. Follow me." He began to climb up the ladder. Marlite didn't move. She looked down toward the boy.

"Jat, go out the window," he said.

The boy ignored him.

"I have said I will not eat this one," said Marlite.

"There will be no fight, Marlite. I will go with you. It is better for all. But first let this beaten giant show you what is at the top of the ladder."

"That sounds bad for me and good for you."

"No, Marlite. It is good for you and good for me. I said I will go with you if that is of your wish."

The other giant gave a quick sniff. "Your words smell of truth. You go up, and I will follow."

There was barely room for the two of them on the top platform. She eyed the farlooker attached to a large, tilted chair. "This is the thing Pryat spoke of? The . . . faraway seeker, yes?"

"Yes," said Newton.

"This holygiant wishes to see what this thing does."

"Are you not afraid the Makers will smite you with skyfire?"

Marlite considered this. "I speak to the Makers on most days and most nights. They know this holygiant."

"Come, then," said Newton. "Sit in this seat and bring your eye to the *glassss*."

"You will not attack me?"

"No, I will not. You speak in truth. I speak in truth."

Marlite sat down in the chair, cautiously eyeing her once-friend. She turned toward the farlooker and placed her eye up to the lens. The giantess drew in a deep breath. She turned to Newton and then back again to the farlooker.

"These are the stars in the sky? They are as suns!"

"Yes," said Newton, tapping the side of the teleoscope. "This makes them come close to our eye, but they are still very far. The stars do not move. The farlooker captures the glow of it and frees it again when I look away. It is in a way take-give, but also in a way it is not. Oh, see this!" He swiveled the chair, aiming the teleoscope toward a faint, glowing area in the distance, and made some adjustments to the lenses. "This is not one fuzzy star. It is many stars joined together by something we cannot see. Something pulls them together, much as the land pulls us to the ground. Each one is as our sun. Our sun warms our lands. Do other suns warm other lands? They could be the Makers' lands, or they could of a chance be more lands of giants. Or mans and womans. Or serpents of the sea. This is what Newton dreams of when he sits in that chair."

"They would be heavy. Why do they not fall from the sky?" asked Marlite.

"I am thinking each one holds the other in place with a kind of pulling or pushing breath, but that is just a fool's guess. In truth, this giant does not know."

Marlite remained silent. "More," she said. Newton knew where to look, having traveled so long through the night sky. The holygiant marveled at what he showed her.

"I will show you one more thing," said Newton. He swung the farlooker, aiming it at an area above the Fire Sea, and pulled back the magnification. "What is this?"

"The Makers' Dragon!" whispered Marlite. She looked at Newton. "How can this be? We are so far from home."

"Do you remember my words on the mountain? Our sky is their sky. Their sky is our sky. We are in the same land under the same sky. The mans call it *world*. There are just many boot-steps between us. When this giant came here, the skyfire fell as it did in our land. As it should under a sky we share. But look. It is not a dragon. They are just stars in the shape of one. Climb down and come outside with me.

"Jat, stay here," said Newton when they reached the bottom. The giants stepped out into the night air, now lit only by the glow of the firetide.

"The skyfire no longer falls. It is over. Remember, Marlite. Our sky is their sky. If the skyfire does not fall here, it does not fall in our land. And how can a dragon breathe skyfire when a dragon is nothing but a gathering of stars?"

Marlite pondered this. She looked Newton in the eye and then returned her gaze to the sky, arching her back to the limit to give her a wider view. There was no skyfire.

"If this is true, you do not anger the Makers. To bring

you to the Iron Thorn would be . . . wrong. THAT would anger the Makers."

Newton heaved a loud sigh of relief. "Yes, Marlite. And, oh! There is more to see!" He wanted her to see his talking wall, especially now that it was dark enough for the Fire Sea flames to make it dance. Marlite, looking at the distant sky, did not notice what was on the cliffs behind her.

"The others come soon," she said.

"This giant knows. Turn and look at the wall, Marlite."

The holygiant studied his face, seeking a trap, and then did as he asked. She gasped in alarm and stumbled away. In front of her was Pryat. Her friend of old had his hand raised in greeting. His arm flickered back and forth, waving that hand.

Unconsciously, Marlite's hand raised in response. "Pryat! You live?"

"No," said Newton. "Look." He reached out and placed his hand on the wall. "It is flat. Newton made this. It is what mans call *drrawing*."

"It is what holygiants call magic," said Marlite sternly. "You are not of a place to do such things, Broo—Newton. Bad things will happen."

Newton tipped his head to the side, puzzled. "What bad things?"

"You, who have been chased and burned and beaten, have to ask this?"

"Good comes from this, Marlite. This is not magic. Mans do this, and they do not have magic. It is how they speak of their lives when they are not there to do it with their mouths. This giant would show you more. Come."

Newton walked farther up the beach. Marlite stayed put a moment longer, leaning in more closely to study the image of Pryat.

"It is him, but it is not him," she said. "Pryat?" She was met with silence.

"If you are waiting for him to speak, that much he cannot do." *But could there be a way this giant doesn't know?* He wished he had the time to figure that out.

Newton walked a distance, searching the wall for a particular image.

"Oh, here it is. Look! What do you see?"

Marlite caught up and leaned forward. Her jaw fell open, and she straightened up. She looked silently, aghast, at Newton, and then leaned back toward the image.

"How?" was all she could manage.

Newton's smile nearly took up his whole face. "With the rocks I find in the sand. Some of them make marks when you scratch them on other rocks."

"But it is of a time that has left us. A giant cannot grow more *young . . . less old.* But . . ." She leaned back in. In front of her was a picture of three giantlings. "This one is you," said Marlite. "This one is young Pryat, and this one . . ." She turned to Newton.

"Is you, Marlite. How can a giant tell his story without his friends and enemies of times past?"

"But there I am a giantling. Here," she said, patting her chest, "I am not."

"You are not a true giantling on the wall. This giant made scratches that *look* to be a young Marlite. The light from the Fire Sea puts shadows on the wall, and the little giants move.

• 186 •

But they do not move, in truth. This giant might have said too soon that mans do not have magic. This feels of magic."

"Dangerous magic, Newton. Newt—" Marlite held out her arm. She was turning.

"No, Marlite! Do not turn! There is nothing to fear! Look!" The giant patted the images with both hands. "It is just a wall with rock scratches. You are real. These are not."

The holygiant took a few long, deep breaths. She staved off the turning.

"Lands in the sky! Giants on walls! I like none of this," she said, scratching her arm.

"Do these make you remember things? They do that for this giant. It is why he makes them."

Marlite looked back at the three young giants. Her features softened a bit. "This giantess does remember this. These were of an earlier time."

"And they were of a good time," said Newton.

"And they were of a good time," said Marlite.

"We would make jest of Pryat. He would not even know until you and I could not stop laughing."

Marlite smiled. "Then he would thrump us both into the ground."

"We would laugh so hard our tears would make mud in the dirt. But then this giant would be of a regret for laughing at our friend. Not because of the thrumping, but because . . . he was slower of thought than you and me."

"Not always," said Marlite. "There were things he spoke of that would surprise this giantess. He just kept more of it inside. He just did what we always told YOU to do."

Marlite explored the talking wall, pausing often to run

her fingers across the images. She looked at her hand. Blue powder from one of the rocks covered her fingertips.

"They bleed, too?"

"No. Just rock dust."

"Magic rock dust?"

"No. Just rock dust."

Then she came across an image that made her stop in her tracks. It was the Iron Thorn. Standing on top of the platform was the giant who stood behind her now. Lightning zigzagged from dark shaded clouds and struck the giant on the wall. Marlite froze and turned to Newton.

"It is all right," said her old friend.

"No, Newton. It is not. I should not have told Mother Shepherd about you watching the Makers."

"If there were Makers up there, this giant did not see them. How did you know?"

"Pryat. He did not speak of it to have you punished. He asked me about what you told him you were seeing. You had the boots in his head walking in circles and circles. Many circles, even for Pryat. He thought a holygiant would know of your stars. This holygiant brought his words to Mother Shepherd. For the same reason, Newton. Not to send you . . ." She pointed silently at the drawing.

"What did she tell you?"

"I am of a thought you know very well. She said that you were spying on the Makers. That they send skyfire to punish us. That the only way to quiet them was to send you to speak with them—to answer for your prying. To stop the skyfire."

"You did not know," said Newton. "No giant could know."

"*You* did!"

"That took a very long time, Marlite. This giant is still learning. This was not of your failing."

"But it was! When the time came for a vote in the Holygiant Chamber to send you to the Thorn, this giantess did not cast a vote of no. All had to say yes, or all had to say no. One no would have saved you. But . . . this giantess believed what Mother Shepherd had told her. We are . . . *trained* to believe what she says. To *do* what she says. Those who do not learn from her die when the time comes for the Makers to speak to us. But if I said no when all the others said yes, you would not have been through this. You would be home. Living back with Ooda . . ."

"*Haroomph!* This giant should *thank* you, then!"

"My truest regrets, Newton. Will you accept them? You do not have to."

"This giant accepts your regrets, Marlite."

"Do you . . . still feel the Makers' Voice in you?"

"No," lied the giant. "There is no pain."

· TWENTY-TWO ·
A Sandgnat's Drop

They returned to Newton's house. Jat was pacing the floor.

"Are you two friends again? Did you figure out what we're doing?"

Marlite looked at the boy and licked her lips. "You do not eat these?" she asked.

"No!" said Newton. "They are giants as we are giants, but not of our size. We do not eat giants! We do not eat mans!"

"Okay. Okay," said the holygiant. "Newton, you must go to find Pryat! You must leave before the others come."

"This giant is happy you will let him."

"I could stop you?"

"Maybe yes," said Newton, sizing up the giantess. They'd been evenly matched when they played as giantlings. But they were no longer giantlings. And she had magic. "But again, maybe no."

Suddenly, Marlite's braid whipped up from behind her

and coiled tightly around Newton's neck, freezing him in place. She gasped. The silver band around her head glowed with white light.

"You lied! The Makers' words still consume you!"

"Yes, Marlite."

"I can take the words away, Newton! Did you not know that?"

"No. I did not. How?"

Marlite closed her eyes. Newton's body tingled and burned as if a nest of cliff-ants had fanned out and stung him at the same time. He could not move. The room took on the fresh, biting smell of an oncoming storm. *Is she doing this to me? Has she grown this strong?* Her body convulsed and then went still. The holygiant opened her eyes. Bright white jagged lines, like lightning, flickered in them and then faded into darkness. She reached into her robes and pulled out a clay vial. "Oh, and *maybe* no? I think maybe *yes*," she said hoarsely. "If I were to command you to drink this, you would do so without question. Tell me this is true."

"It is true," said the giant. He would do anything she told him. His will was hers. *How does she do this? It is her braid!* He tried to take it back. To say it was *not* true. He could not.

Marlite smiled impishly. "And if this giantess was to tell you to . . . rub noses with her, Newton would do so without question. Tell me this is true."

"Stop this!" shouted Jat.

"Quiet, boy!" spat Newton.

The holygiant's braid unwound itself from Newton's neck, and she stumbled back. There was a weariness to her face that had not been there moments before. Newton rubbed his throat.

"You have learned new tricks since becoming a holygiant," he said, his voice sounding raw.

"Many," she said. "It is a thing you should know. How is your pain?"

Newton hugged his body. The pain he had lived with for so long was . . . gone! It was a thing he had grown so used to, he'd forgotten what it felt like to be free of it.

"How did you . . . What did you do to me?" he asked.

"I silenced the Makers," said Marlite. "They scream inside me now, but They will leave in time. You were carrying great pain, Newton. This would have burned through the hearts of most giants. In short time you would have been brought to stone. It is of a wonder you had not turned yet!"

Newton felt such a wave of relief it was hard to breathe. It overwhelmed him. It was almost as strong as the pain itself.

"You can chase away the Makers' words in a giant?"

"Yes," answered Marlite.

"This giant is grateful," he said. "You will be all right?"

"In time. All holygiants must learn to carry the Makers' words. We have all stood on the Thorn. It is why many fail to live through training. I will carry this for some time and release it slowly. If I do it too fast, there will be pieces of me scattered throughout the land."

"Do you not feel the pain of it?"

"Oh, I do," said Marlite. "But a giantess can bear pain better than a giant. But yes. It hurts very much."

"It is my regret."

"It makes a little smaller this giantess's regret, Newton. So a balance is made?"

"Your balance is made," said Newton. He pointed to the vial. "What is that?"

"It is stoneturner oil. If fear did not turn you, this would. A stone giant does not punch or kick," she said. "A stone giant goes where carried."

"Would it work on me?" asked Jat.

"Why would my friend ask this? *Foomph* . . . Oh, yes, this giant can answer his own question."

"Rocks don't burn in the Fire Sea. I see them in the tide all the time. If she gave me some of this, you could carry me in your pocket. I could go with you."

"I am not of ease with that thought, Jat," said the giant.

"I want to try it," said the boy. "How does it work? Do you drink it?"

"You are fond of this pet mans?" Marlite asked Newton.

"Jat is not my pet. He is this giant's friend."

"Yes," said Marlite to the boy. "But for you, I would give just a sandgnat's drop. And even that might be of too great a dose." She looked at the boy, studying him more closely. "*Hoomph*, it may not work at all. It may even take its little life away."

"Let's do it. We have to go, Newton. We can't argue about this."

"No."

"Yes. Stop questioning everything I say. I am always right."

Newton laughed. "That is not true."

"I am this time."

"I do not like this, Jat. What if you do not turn back? What if it . . . kills my friend?"

"I'm almost dead already, remember?" said the boy, smiling. "Compared to you, at least. It is my choice. I want to help you find your friend. I want to see the other lands, the other seas. I can help you if you help me! A giant stands with his friends. You said that to me once, remember? Well, so does a man. Carry your friend through the Fire Sea!"

Newton turned to Marlite. "When will this wear off? What if he turns back while we are still in the Fire Sea?"

Marlite shrugged. "For a giant, a large swallow makes him stone for half a moon cycle. It took us that time to walk beneath the flames. For a . . . little giant, I do not know. And his blood smells not as ours. I do not know how it will mix."

"Can I see it?" asked Jat. The holygiant set the vial on the floor. It was nearly as tall as the boy. He pushed off the cap and peered inside. "A sandgnat, eh?" he said, dipping his finger in. He pulled it out again. A drop sat like a golden bead on his fingertip. "How big are your sandgnats?"

"Do not do this," said Newton. "We will think of another way."

"No time," he said, and put the finger in his mouth.

"Do NOT!" shouted the giant.

Jat looked up at him and then back down to his body. "It didn't work," he said.

"GOOD!" said Newton. "I do not like the danger of this! I am of a thought to enclose you in a stone box, like the one that carried my *boooks* across the sea. I might have one in here I can use." The giant lumbered across the room and began rifling through his things. *The pain! The pain is gone!* "The box will stop the heat, I am thinking." Then he paused. "But what if it does not? No, this is a very bad idea . . . and I have no stone box . . ."

"It doesn't matter," said Marlite.

"How can it not matter?" asked Newton.

"Your pet turned."

TWENTY-THREE

Beneath the Fire Sea

"They come," said Marlite. "Take the tiny giant and run. And here..." The holygiant reached into a pocket and pulled out a smaller vial. She poured a couple of drops of the oil into it and handed it to him. "If it starts to turn while in the fire, give it more, but not much more. I am of a thought I should hold on to the rest, though."

Newton took the vial and put it in his pocket. "What do I do when we reach the wet sea?"

"Remember, Newton. We have our tree stacks waiting. They are tied to Gossan. This giantess asks that you do not take them all, though. She does wish to return home."

"I am thinking there will be one extra," said the giant. "Flintoak will not be returning."

"You felled him?"

"No, a mans did—Constable Stoggin."

"One of those little things?" she asked, pointing to Jat.

"Yes."

Marlite looked impressed and then concerned. "Go, Newton."

"What will you tell the Council?" asked Newton.

"I will tell them you ran into the flames. Newton, go!" pleaded the holygiant.

"Will they believe you?"

"I am of a hope that when they see the skyfire falls no more they will think the Makers appeased. And the hunt will end. It should end. We have made you suffer enough."

"Crag would not agree. The hunt will not end for him."

"No. He would not, and no, it will not."

"I could stay, then. And show them myself," said Newton.

"Good giants and an Apooncha died chasing you. The holygiants will end their hunt for you, but you still want to be far from Crag and Aphanfel. And from Greyelm the most far. Go!"

Newton touched his fist to his chest and bowed his head in gratitude.

"This giant praises the kind act of a holygiant," he said. He picked up Jat and gently placed him in his other pocket. He turned back to Marlite, about to say something else, but lost his nerve. The giant heaved a sigh and ran out the door.

Newton clomped across the beach. If he entered the Fire Sea and traveled in a straight line from where the other giants had emerged, he was of a hope he would come close to where the tree jumbles waited. He found what he thought to be the right spot and waded into the tide of flames. Only when he was below the surface did he slow his pace. They couldn't see him, so they would have no idea he was going after Pryat. *Will they believe Marlite?* If they did not believe he left, they would keep searching for him, and soon they would find mans. *Will she be punished for letting me go?* He hoped she could convince them that the danger was over. They had to see the skyfire had ended. He found himself thinking about the holygiant. She had never been cruel to him, even as giantlings, when most giantesses had yet to outgrow their berserker stage. Although some, like his sister, never did. He reached back in his memory and recalled Marlite's scent. Her blood always smelled of *knowing things*, far more than most giants. But she smelled of something else, too, as she did today. It was the crisp, cold, wet-leaves smell of magic. She was becoming a powerful holygiant, powerful beyond her piddling years. *She healed me! She took my pain and made it hers!* Newton wondered if he was still partially under her spell. He could not stop picturing her face. Her nose. That great rockbeet of a nose . . . *Now I am wishing she escaped with me.* But it was too late to turn back. And she had to get them to call off their search for him back on land. *She also let them send me up the Thorn*, he reminded himself.

The giant felt his pocket. Jat was still solid rock. He would have to check often to quickly stave off his turning should it happen too soon. Marlite had told him that the oil lasted about half a moon cycle. That was also about how long it had taken them to travel the floor of the Fire Sea. Newton sighed. He had a long, hard journey ahead. *It does not end*, he thought. *Giants chase. Newton runs. And so it goes.*

And so it went . . . Many creatures dwelled below the surface, some he'd encountered on his way toward the land of peoples. Most floated through the flames on bodies filled with hot air. It was a discovery he made upon eating them. They did little to sate his hunger and gave him terrible gas. One fish looked like a mushroom pulling a thousand dangling, stringy legs. It stung his tongue when he put it in his mouth. *These, I will need more of!* A school of glowing eels wriggled by him, changing color with every flick of the tail. The giant turned and saw they were being chased by what looked to be a large tongue of flame. Bubbling eyes floated above its luminous gaping blue mouth. He stepped aside to let it pass.

The giant plodded on. A week into his journey saw little change. He thought often about Theobold's journal, which he had read many times back home. And, of course, the book Flora had given him. The one he'd given up for lost. He absently reached into his pocket and pulled it out. It went up in a puff of smoke.

"NO! What an OX I am!" cried Newton. *Another boook— the same one, even, food for the flames!* He patted his friend through his pocket, promising himself not to show such carelessness again. *There can be no room for empty thoughts. Not yet. This was a good lesson.*

"A lost *boook* for a safe friend." He sighed. "Halfway there." *This giant hopes.*

Night and day became one long, continuous stretch of time. There was no rising and setting sun. No stars or moonlit sky. Everything flickered and shimmered in a haze of yellow and orange. Newton passed the time speaking to Jat. He knew the boy could not hear him, but it felt good to tell someone about his life—of times of joy, of times of sadness. He spoke of battles won and battles lost, of giant legends and lands of wild. He was of a need to share such things. It was a need once filled by his talking wall back home. His old home. His *other* old home . . .

During the brief moments he stopped to rest, he scratched drawings of the things he'd seen into the sandy floor of the Fire Sea. He knew they wouldn't last long, but it felt good to do something that had become familiar to him.

In time the fire grew thicker—heavier. *It is starting to change.* He pushed his weary legs forward. It was becoming harder to breathe. How would he get to the surface when it became liquid? At last he was forced to stop. He had finally reached the edge. If he kept going, his lungs would fill with boiling water. He would drown, as would Jat, if he turned back.

"I would be grateful for your ideas now, Jat," he said, his words barely escaping his mouth. He paced the undulating border where the Fire Sea met the red, liquid sea, looking for a tunnel, a bridge, anything to ease the journey between the two. How were the other giants going to return? They must have a plan. *Marlite,* he thought. *Holygiant magic.* Even more now, he wished she had escaped with him.

"I have come so far and now it ends here?" Fury flashed through his body. He dropped to his knees and pounded the sandy floor. The vial of stoneturner oil slipped from his pocket. The stopper was knocked free and the droplets of oil rolled out, instantly igniting into yellow sparks. If Jat turned now, there would be nothing he could do. He would be forced to watch his friend go out in a flash of fire, just as the boy had watched happen to *his* father.

"THIS MUST END!" he shouted. His lungs filled with roiling red liquid. He choked and rolled away from the edge of the thick crimson water, back to where it was still mostly flames. The giant coughed and retched violently, nearly turning his empty stomach inside out. The spasms subsided and he sat, head between his knees, forcing himself to breathe. He felt sick in the belly; the red water was of a poison to him. He felt it bubbling inside his lungs. Newton looked up and flinched. The back of his neck tingled, signaling the onset of turning to stone. "NO!" he demanded. The sound of his own crackling voice was enough to shake it off. He was in control. He would not turn. He retched again, bringing up more of the noxious fluid. When he was done, he looked ahead through the bright haze. There, rippling in the current, stood a giant. He could barely make him out in the distance, but Newton knew who it was.

"Gossan."

He was as Marlite said he would be. Solid stone, feet sunken into the seafloor. A tangle of ropes wrapped around his waist were stretched taut up to the glimmering surface. *Did they turn him to Everstone for this? Or did he do it to himself?* Newton would like to think that as desperate as the giants were to capture him, they would not have resorted to killing one of their party. The laws forbade it. *Would Marlite have allowed this?*

Newton touched his pocket. "Just a little longer," he said to his friend. "This is of a challenge . . ."

The giant stared at Gossan. There was no question he was in the watery side of the Fire Sea border. Giants don't float, so even if Newton made it to him, he'd be as trapped as the poor creature holding the tree stacks in place. The thought of plunging into a liquid sea started him turning once again. Then he remembered something Jat had said long ago when discussing this.

"And turning to stone makes the fear come true. You are stuck, aren't you? You're afraid a real thing is going to happen, and the real thing happens because you are afraid."

"Yes, Jat. This is of an odd truth," Newton had said. *"It seems that if half of this is made to go away, the whole trouble will follow."*

Newton calmed his thoughts. He would not *turn* in fear of a thing that may not happen. *Thank you, Jat. You* were *here to help this giant!*

He looked back at Gossan. What was keeping him from being pulled away by the floating vessels? He took a deep breath of thick, fiery air and crossed over for a better look. The surrounding air quickly turned liquid. It was still very hot, but no longer breathable. He reached the stone giant. *A question answered,* he thought. *Foot is hooked on a rock!* He looked up and saw the dark shapes of the trees above. There were seven tangles of them. One for each giant, including the dead Puncher, himself, and an extra one that was twice the size of the others. *Why is there one more than they need?*

The ropes were too thin and slippery for a giant to climb without a foothold. It didn't matter. He had another idea.

He crossed back to the flaming side of the Fire Sea and took a deep breath. Newton plunged back into the molten water toward the stone giant. He looked at Gossan's face and instantly regretted it. The large giant had not turned peace-fully. All he had to do now was free his foot from the rock and grab on tight. The mass of trees would be set loose, carrying him with them. But he would still have to climb the ropes. And it would leave Marlite with no way to return home. *Why should this giant care so much? She chased me here!*

...But she also took on my pain...Foomph, thought Newton. *Now what?*

He was running out of time. Every moment it took to get to the surface was a moment bringing Jat closer to flesh. The boy was out of the fire now and into the boiling water. He had another idea. *This will have to work.*

He climbed onto Gossan and wrapped his legs around his waist. The giant reached up, grabbed two of the ropes, and pulled. The tree stacks sank a few feet below the surface. It was not as much as he had hoped. He wrapped the rope around his hand so he would not lose what he'd gained. He pulled again, harder, straining the muscles in his arms and shoulders beyond their limit. He heard a *pop. Not good*, thought Newton. It was his left shoulder, already injured from his clash with Crag. *Or the fall from the mountain.* Still he pulled on the ropes, hand over hand. Pull, wrap, wrap, pull, wrap, wrap... The timbers fought to escape to the surface. Pull, wrap, wrap, pull, wrap, wrap...

The exertion ate up all the giant's air. If he didn't finish soon, he'd have to give up and race back to the flames, and then start all over. He didn't know if he'd be able to get this close again. His strength was spent. His shoulder was grow-ing useless.

Something twitched in his pocket. *Jat! NO!* He pulled

with all his might. The tree stacks descended one painful foot at a time. When they were just within reach, he unhooked his legs from the stone giant. The timbers shot up through the water, dragging him behind. They exploded onto the surface. Newton kept going. His head smashed through one of the jumbles of trees, splintering it to pieces. He gasped for air, clawing wildly for something to keep him afloat. Realizing he was still holding the ropes, he gave them another pull and brought one of the timbers closer to him. He hung his arms over the side and paddled to a nearby vessel. With his very last reserve of strength, he pulled himself aboard and collapsed.

· TWENTY-FOUR ·

Blue, Red, Black, White, Nothing

When he awoke, Jat was standing in front of his face. The boy scratched vigorously at his sides.

"I thought you'd never wake up," he said. "I'm itchy all over. Does that happen to you?"

The giant sighed in relief. "Yes, Jat. It will wear off. I am glad you are back to yourself."

"How about this?" he asked. He held up his left hand. It was still stone.

"Hrmmm . . ." said Newton. "That should not be."

"Didn't think so. It's okay, though. I made it! Having a rock hand is worth it."

"I hope so, Jat. Is everything else back to normal?"

"I think so," said the boy. "Except the water is red—and screaming hot! It's like that melted glass we made. But it's not fire anymore. It's not burning the raft."

Newton sat up and stretched. His shoulder popped. It sounded like a cannon shot. "*Oomph*," he said, wincing. "That hurt."

"Are you all right?" asked Jat.

"Shoulders heal. No, it is not of a heat that burns wood. Or at least wood from a giant's land."

"Well, that's good, because it's of a heat that burns me."

The giant surveyed his surroundings. There were six tree stacks still moored to the stone giant below. Each consisted of large cobbletrees—stacked crisscrossed and lashed together by strong vines. A huge wooden enclosure sat on one of them. He thought he heard sounds coming from it. *Moo?*

"Cows, it sounds like, yes? But a little more rumbly than cows," said the boy. "I think your friends brought lunch for the trip back. I wish they cooked them first."

"That is a mans thing, not a giants thing."

"I know. I know."

Far on the horizon spun the waterspout. It was where they'd be heading. But how would they get there against the current? *First thing before next thing*, thought the giant. He was hungry. Newton pulled the rope attached to the huge beast-bearing raft until it bumped into his own. He stepped onto the deck and looked down into the wooden corral. Fourteen oxen looked up at him. The giants had left the animals with enough food and water to keep them alive until their return. He heaved one out. "They are not the fattest of oxes. But . . . It is my regret, ox. Thank you, ox," he said, and bit it in half, the head half first, always, to make it quicker for the animal. Newton moaned in delight. He finished that one and then he ate two more. The giant looked down at Jat, covered in spray from the constricted intestines of his meal. The boy looked sick to his stomach.

"I know you do not eat live animals," he said, "but it might be of a time to start."

"No thanks," said Jat. "I think they will cook in this water, though. Could you . . . ?"

Newton knew what he asked. He pulled out an ox. "It is my regret, ox. Thank you, ox." He bit off its head with a merciful chomp and held it in the hot water until it was cooked.

"Thanks," said Jat. "You know, they don't understand what you are saying to them."

"I am not an oaf, Jat. I know this. They do not understand, but this giant does."

"Well, this . . . shoub . . . hobe me for a goob long tibe," he said through a mouthful of boiled ox. He swallowed. "Speaking of which . . . let's go! It's hot here—real hot! For me, at least. I'm surprised those cows are still alive."

"The oxes are of my land. They do not suffer heat in the way of mans and womans ox cows, I am of a guess. Unless you dip them in this red . . . water-but-not-water. We have to get to the twisting sea and join the ice stream. It is where I am told Pryat went. But a jumble of trees cannot move against the water that pushes it back."

"Have you ever heard of a sail?"

"I have not."

"The fishermen use them to travel the oceans in my world. They take a big sheet, like, say, your shirt, and hang it from a mast, like, say, these logs floating around us. The wind blows the sheet, which pulls the ship. I've tried it before. Not very good at it, but I got it to move my little boat."

Newton's face lit up! "It is like the seeds that ride the wind!"

The giant fished a couple of the smaller trees from the water, remnants of the craft he had smashed when he burst to the surface. He and Jat lashed them together with rope from the destroyed vessel and attached his shirt by sliding the sleeves over the crosspiece. There was no way to attach it to the raft, so Newton held it in place, sitting cross-legged in the middle. A board torn from the ox enclosure would be used as a rudder.

"Just keep turning it until it picks up the breeze," said Jat. "It'll puff out with air when you get the right spot."

"How did you learn this?" asked Newton.

"I fish in the harvest season, remember? In a boat. In the water. Seen others do it. Tried it, but without a giant's shirt. I'm burning up, Newton. I'm used to Fire Sea heat, but this is too much. I know what too much is! Come on!"

Newton's shirt caught the wind and billowed out like an enormous jellyfish. "I have the wind!" he shouted. "I HAVE IT!" He laughed so hard he quaked the entire raft.

"Great! Don't let it go! Now we drop the rudder in and steer. That's my job. And it'll keep me behind you, out of the hot spray."

"Do not fall in!" warned the giant.

"Really? I thought I would enjoy a swim!"

"NO! DO NOT . . . Oh . . ."

The giant and the boy flew across the surface. Newton roared with excitement. "No giant has done this!"

Jat laughed. "You're doing just fine, giant! We're aiming straight for the waterspout, right?"

"Yes. Once we are close, we will not need the wind. The current will take us—at least I am of that thought."

They sailed for the rest of the day. The breeze was strong and carried them a good distance. The waterspout soon loomed before them. To Newton, it looked like a tangle of vines lashing about a heavy, twisting stalk. It was a fearsome sight. *It moves as if alive. And of anger.* He wondered, as he had the first time he approached it, if this could be a way to escape the sea. It was surely large enough to lend boothold to a full thunder of giants. He looked up to where it disappeared into a spinning mass of clouds. How long would he be climbing until he reached a place to stop? But he knew this was not a plant but a tunnel of air and water. The enormous waterspout, a sickly gray-green mass, spun, anchored by its tail to a raging whirlpool. Whatever it drew from the sea fed the murky clouds above.

"It looks like a big tree," said Jat.

"It does."

Newton lowered the mast and slid his shirt off the crossbeam. He laid the logs on the floor of the vessel should they need the wind's help again once they set on their new path.

The current was rapidly drawing them toward the vortex. The whirlpool at the base now demanded their attention. It pulled them toward a churning blend of fire, ice, blue ocean, blackness, and . . . nothing. A ribbon of *nothingness*, an absence of anything at all. The thought of it always clawed at Newton's insides.

"What *is* that?" shouted Jat. "Or what *isn't* that?"

"It isn't *something*."

The roar of the currents added to the deafening howl of the whirlwind. "Do you smell that?" shouted Newton.

The surging streams pummeled them and their craft, switching directions from one blink to the next. They held on tightly to the lashing.

"No," shouted Jat.

"I don't know what it is, but it is not new to this giant's nose."

"Thanks! I really needed to know that," yelled the boy.

"I will steer now," shouted the giant. "The water will pull hard."

"Is your shoulder all right?"

"It will be. Is your hand still . . . ?"

Jat rapped it on the log. "Still a rock."

Newton breathed in deeply. "Does Jat smell that now?"

The boy sniffed. "No."

"It smells of . . . everything. Of everything that is!"

They approached the foot of the swirling gray column of water. The surface broke into a pinwheel of colors, each maybe leading, Newton thought, to a different destination.

"What is that black one?" asked Jat.

"I do not know," said Newton. He pointed to the blue-green stripe. "I know only the one that leads to my home. That one. We want the white, icy one."

"I wonder where it goes."

I am of a hope to Pryat.

Their craft picked up more speed as they drew nearer to the center of the whorling eddy. Newton held them steady as the water changed beneath them. Ice scraped against the timbers. The raft groaned loudly.

"NOW!" shouted Jat.

The giant wrapped his arms around the board and swept it across the water trailing in their wake. The raft turned hard; it picked up the current and was wrenched away from the vortex. The ice-choked course took charge of their destination. Newton and Jat each breathed a sigh of relief.

"And off we go," said the boy.

"And off we go," said the giant.

· TWENTY-FIVE ·
The Ice Sea

The air was cold, colder than Jat was dressed for. The boy denied it, but Newton was pretty sure mans weren't supposed to shake so much. He tore the edge from his sleeve and tossed it over him.

"Why did you do that?"

"Make a cloak to keep warm. Your teeth click like a sand cricket."

Several days of floating on the icy current brought them to a vast white sea. The raft moved slowly, sometimes so slowly it felt as if they were moving backward. Jat assured Newton that they were not.

"Point your eyes on the star in the north, the one in the handle of the smaller spoon, or *Baby* Dragon."

"We will call it the Dragon's Whelp."

Jat laughed. "Ha! Okay, now just hold your thumb under it and you'll see it moves away from it, after a while. My dad showed me that. I don't think it's moving. We are."

"I do see that," said Newton. "I am learning to listen to the stars when they speak."

Jat pulled another chunk of meat from his ox. At least the cold kept the meat from spoiling.

"You should have brought the raft of oxen," he said.

"I would not leave the giants with no food. I took my fill. I will be all right."

"You mean you won't leave *Marlite* with no food."

Newton's face turned pale blue. "Her too."

"What if we are stuck here for weeks—or months?"

The giant rubbed his chin as if he were pondering the question. "Well then, my 'pet,' I will do as giants do. I will eat you."

Jat stopped chewing. His face turned serious. Then he laughed. He stood up and grabbed the giant's finger, twisting it back. "You will have to defeat me in battle first! I will pound you with my hand of stone!"

Now Newton laughed. "Jat is a Puncher! Okay! Okay! You win! Please do not eat ME!"

The days and nights slid by with little to do but sleep, talk, and stare out at the sea and sky. One night, as they were lying back looking up at the stars, the same stars that were in each of their homelands, Jat asked a question he had promised to never ask again.

"Newton? I know you don't want to talk about this, but you once said you might tell me what happened to your mother and father? I only ask because it seems to really make you mad, or sad, or both, and sometimes, I think, not telling anyone makes it worse."

"Like you not telling me about the Fengiss brothers?"

"I know I was mad when you found out, but after that, I wasn't. I was actually a little glad. I don't know . . . With some people, *not* saying things is harder than saying them. But you just get used to keeping your mouth shut."

The giant remained silent for a long time.

"Okay. Never mind," said Jat. "I won't ask again."

"No," said Newton. "It is okay. I am just not proud of what I did. You were not the cause of what happened to your father. It is different."

"Never mind. Really," said Jat. "I'm going to try for some more fish . . ."

"I learned about the shadow that hides the moon. My *boooks* showed me that my land is round, like a giant's eye. This *world* is round. When the sun slips behind it, its shadow is put on the moon and the moon grows dark."

"That happens every year," said Jat. "Some people go crazy. They think the moon is being eaten by some giant something. Not the *you* kind of giant, but one in the sky. Hey, maybe it's one of your Makers!"

"*Hoomph* . . . I should not laugh . . ."

"But then the moon comes back and everyone forgets about it until next time."

"Yes. The giants say, *the few that notice* say, 'The Makers feed. If their belly is not filled by the moon, they turn their hunger on us.' But they never do. We giants are forever in fear of angering the *fo fum* Makers. But I, too, believed that to be true until I learned of our land's great shadow on the moon. One night, I looked up and saw the shadow would come. When much of your time is passed looking at the sky, you sometimes know what comes and when it will come. *You* know this. The shadow was at the edge of the moon. I thought to use it for my own humor. I pulled Mother and Father out behind our home to show them 'Newton's great magic.' It was a trick. I told them I was going to . . . eat the moon. There was jest in my words and humor in their hearts . . . They laughed." Newton stopped, recalling their laughter. Jat said nothing. They looked up at the quarter moon in the night sky.

"I think I know what happened," said the boy finally.

"I am of a thought you do not, Jat. I said to them, 'Behold your son. He has the power to swallow the moon! You have bred a great Maker!' And the shadow bit farther into the edge. The bites grew wider, the moon smaller. This giant was so held by the sight of it, he did not turn to see the smiles on his parents' faces. When he did turn . . . there were no smiles. They were stone. The horror of what their son could do, a son with the great powers of the Makers, was more than a parent could bear. If any other had done this, Mother and Father would still be of bone and hide. But that it was their son . . . a Maker—*their* own son. It was a thought to wound a mind—two minds. They cared too much for this fool of a giant. It is frozen on their faces to this day." Newton closed his eyes. "And it is frozen in my heart to this day."

"I can see why it's not something you talk about. I'm sorry, Newton."

"I knew that you would be. It is why I told you."

"Is that why your sister hates you?"

"Ooda cannot understand what I did. Her mind is like that of many giants. It knows what it knows, and it will not know more than that. If what is in a giant's head is enough to keep that giant alive, that is enough. They circle through their lives—loops and loops and loops—doing the same thing over and over because it has yet to kill them. She knows I did not want to hurt our family—that it brings me pain, but she knows that it is a thing I did. I try to make her understand, but she just pulls my ears."

"So . . . are they, your parents, are they stuck like that forever? Won't they turn back? You always did. Even I did . . ."

"Yes, Jat. Everstone is forever a time lasting. It can come from more than one way. Gossan is Everstone because he can never leave the red water. He can never escape from the thing that turns him. But it can come also from a fear deeper than the loss of a giant's own life. It can come from the fear of losing one a giant . . . loves . . . loves more than their own hide. My parents gave their own selves to the love of this foolish giant. And when they believed gone the Newton who carried that love, they, too, went. They feared a great fear of what the Makers had made me . . . What it would do to me. To them, this giant was gone . . . because of my jest of humor . . ."

"But, Newton, how is it you were not turned to Everstone? Don't you feel about them what they felt about you?"

"There is a difference between fear and shame, Jat— between fear and sadness. Fear is what turns us. Shame and sadness . . . we live with."

"There has to be something we can do—when we get back there. *If* we get back there."

"Jat is a kind friend, but my land is not for boys. Or

grown mans. It is said that a dragon's fire can turn a stone giant back, but that is just a . . . what do you call them? Goatstories?"

"Nannytales," said the boy.

"Yes, nannytales," sighed the giant.

"You know what?" asked Jat.

"I do not," said Newton.

"Remember what I said when I first met you? *'I thought giants were just monsters in nannytales'*?"

Newton laughed. "I do remember that."

"Well, here you are."

Several weeks passed on their journey across the vast and frigid expanse of ocean—the "Ice Sea," they'd come to call it. Jat's ox was nearly devoured. Newton refused to eat any of it. As hungry as he was, he was revolted by the thought of eating a cooked animal. The boy had managed to carve fishhooks from one of the bones. He was getting the hang of using one hand. The other one became more of a brace for whatever he was working on. Thread from the giant's pants made strong lines. He baited the hooks with oxmeat and hung them over the edge of the raft to trail behind them. They caught the occasional fish, something to tease the empty stomach of his large friend. It wasn't enough, but Newton was grateful for every bite. The giant silently hoped for a sea serpent to rear its head. With the mast still aboard the raft, he had a weapon with which to take one down, but none appeared. *Maybe it is too cold for big snakes.*

Every few days brought a blizzard of snow, thoroughly

delighting Newton, who thought it was "of a great beauty." Jat made no attempt to hide that he felt otherwise.

"I am so tired of white. White ice. White snow. Even all the fish are white!"

Newton patted his belly. "I will eat every white fish that you can catch. I will eat every black fish that you can catch. I will eat every red fish that you can catch. I will eat—"

"Anything. I got it," said the boy. He looked at the giant's belly. "Is the pain still gone? From the lightning?"

"It is, Jat. Sometimes, though, this giant misses it."

"How can you miss pain?"

"After a time, it becomes something else. It makes other pains less. But this giant is being foolish. He is happy it is gone."

"Well, especially since it was going to kill you—turn you to stone."

"Yes, especially since."

They were beginning to wonder if this sea would ever meet land. Being so low on food, it was a very real worry. The giant's strength was failing. He tried to hide it, but he felt Jat's concerned stares when he wasn't looking. Newton also snuck looks at Jat. He often caught the boy scratching the back of his stone hand. He probably wasn't as unbothered about the change as he let on.

At fifty feet tall, Newton had a pretty good view of the surroundings. The boy stopped asking him if he could see anything. The answer was always the same. The giant stood again to scan the horizon.

"Maybe you're too short," said Jat. "Maybe land is just over the edge of what you can see."

"Maybe yes. But again, maybe no," said Newton. "You can look if you think you can see more far."

Jat kicked the mast at the edge of the raft. "Hey!" he said. "Look!" He ran to the end of the mast and wrapped his arms and legs around it. "Pick this up! We can see twice as *more far*!"

"You will fall."

"No I won't. Just do it."

Newton cocked his head, considering this idea.

"It is heavy. This giant is weak."

"No, it's light, and you are strong!"

"You will hold on tight? Your hand . . ."

"No," said Jat. "I'm going to do a dance on top of it once I get up there. Of course I will hold on tight!"

"You be careful," said the giant, and he reluctantly grabbed the log. It was nearly twice his height and heavy for a giant who'd eaten nothing but tiny fishlings for weeks on end. With a grunt, he hoisted the boy into the air. Jat looked toward the horizon.

"Spin," he called down. "I need a full view all around." Newton turned in a circle.

"Do you see anything?"

"No," said Jat. "Wait . . . no. Wait . . . yes! I see a dot. A tiny dot way back from where we came from."

"What is the dot?" asked Newton. "Is it of a big thing that is far, or a little thing that is close?"

"I don't know. Now I don't see it."

"I am of a thought to pull you down now," said the giant. He started to carefully feed the mast through his arms.

"Wait!" yelled Jat.

"Another dot? I do not like this," said Newton.

"NO!" shouted Jat. "This is different! It's ahead of us, but off to the north more. I see land, but we're going the wrong way!"

Newton brought Jat back down. The boy jumped up and down in excitement.

"It's there! Land! In the north! If we kept going where we were going we would have missed it!"

"Are these words of truth? There is land? Sometimes we see things when we want to see them, but they are as empty wishes."

"Newton. I saw land. We have to set up the sail again. It's only about two, maybe three, days away."

Newton smiled and clapped his hands.

"There are many giants under the great sky, but none as happy as this one."

They quickly lashed together the mast and crossbeam, stripped off the giant's shirt, and set sail north. The raft crashed through the ice, slicing into the lashing that held it together. Neither of them cared. Land was ahead. They would not need a raft once they got there. Newton swore he'd never set foot on one again for as long as he drew breath. Giants were not meant for the sea: the Great Sea, the Fire Sea, the Ice Sea. He had had a bellyful of all of them.

Soon the land came into sight. It appeared to be frozen, as they'd expected. Towering walls of ice rose from the sea from south to north. But there were signs of life. Birds circled overhead, and in time, over their craft. The giant snatched one from the air and tossed it in his mouth.

They had traveled for two days since spotting land. The

breeze died at nightfall, floundering the raft just a few miles from the coast. It was the longest night either of them had ever spent. They were so close! Newton carved images of their journey into the bark of the raft with his fingernail to pass the time.

"My mother doesn't like Bonnie," said Jat, breaking a long silence.

"She was in your thoughts, this giant is guessing?"

"She says she is wild. She gets boys to do what she wants, and it gets them in trouble."

"Why do they do what she wants?" asked Newton.

"You know why," said the boy. "You've seen her."

"With both of my own eyes," said the giant. "Does she have magic? I thought mans had no magic."

Jat laughed. "In a way. She's pretty, Newton, okay?"

"*Harooomph*... Mans' pretty and giants' pretty are of great oceans apart. But she did smell of . . . a wildness. So do you, Jat."

"What does it smell like?"

Newton sniffed. "Field carrots. Field carrots and hot tongue pepper."

"What does Marlite smell like? I mean with your giant nose."

"Time to rest. This giant grows tired."

The wind picked up in the morning, and they continued their mad ride into the waves of the shore. The tree stack's timbers were breaking loose and banged noisily into one another, threatening to crush Jat's feet. Newton was busy holding the sail, so the boy had to keep abandoning the rudder to try to pull the logs together. At last, the vessel, tossed into the jagged ice and rocks at the coast, fell apart.

"NO! This can't be! NOT YET!" cried Jat. The two plunged into the freezing water. The giant grabbed the boy and held him above his head. The water was only up to his chest.

"Sorry I panicked," said the boy.

"Unnoticed," said the giant. He walked the rest of the way and set him down on the rocky shore.

The two stood in silence, taking in this new land. It could easily be either of their homelands. Tall pines edged the cliffs that corralled the shore. The walls of ice were not ice but stone. Newton picked up a chunk that had rolled away from the base. It was soft, and it crushed into powder between his fingers. The air was warm, surprisingly so, considering the frozen sea that surrounded them. Birds sang. A crab crossed Jat's foot, causing him to leap back. He looked up at the giant and laughed.

An earsplitting screech filled the air. The two jumped in alarm. They looked toward the noise, which came from the tops of the pines. A dragon hovered above, body held steady as its great wings shifted in the wind. It studied the two newcomers, tipping its head back and forth as if trying to make sense of what it was seeing. It let loose another screech and then turned and flew away, disappearing beyond the treetops.

Newton stood with mouth agape, silently questioning if what he saw was what he saw. Jat turned and looked up at the giant. He was grinning ear to ear.

"Another nannytale?"

· TWENTY-SIX ·

A Giantess Follows

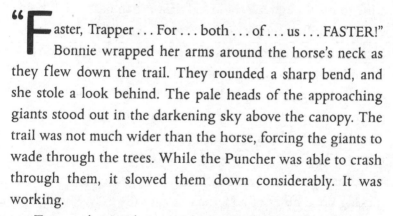

"**F**aster, Trapper . . . For . . . both . . . of . . . us . . . FASTER!"
Bonnie wrapped her arms around the horse's neck as
they flew down the trail. They rounded a sharp bend, and
she stole a look behind. The pale heads of the approaching
giants stood out in the darkening sky above the canopy. The
trail was not much wider than the horse, forcing the giants to
wade through the trees. While the Puncher was able to crash
through them, it slowed them down considerably. It was
working.

Trapper, having been on this path many times, needed no
urging to stay on course. He would make the loop and return
to where he'd started, as he always did. When they made it
back to the barn, Bonnie slowed down to check on her
pursuers.

"I hear them but can't see them. Good job, Trapper!" She

patted the side of the horse's neck. It was soaked in perspiration. "We can't stop yet, boy. I'm so sorry. Just take me to the beach so I can warn Jat. You can rest then."

Marlite watched Newton disappear into the Fire Sea. She went back into his home to wait for the other giants to return. The room was dark. She stepped back outside and found a large shiny stone. It was similar to the *kuwaart* stones back home. The holygiant held it to her forehead. It began to glow a radiant yellow-white, bright enough to dimly illuminate the room. Setting the light on the table, she explored the many scratchings her once-giantling friend had made on the sheets of white bark. "He is a curious one," she muttered. ". . . Brings a life to his thoughts. A bold oaf. But *not* an oaf . . . but bold, yes." She sniffed the images. "*Paroomp*. It smells of him, too." Marlite drew a deep breath. A wisp of a smile formed on her broad lips. She closed her eyes and sniffed it again.

The holygiant stepped back outside and searched the Fire Sea once more. There were only flames. No giants entering them. No giants leaving them. She grimaced in pain and held her ribs. "Do not talk so loud," she ordered the the Makers' Voice inside her. She went back inside and sat against the wall, picking up another of Newton's images to study. She sniffed it and smiled. Soon she dozed.

Marlite was awakened by an itch on her nose. When she opened her eyes, something was tickling her face.

"What did you do to them?" screamed Bonnie. The girl had climbed atop the sleeping giantess and was pounding on her nose. Marlite picked her up and tossed her to the floor.

Bonnie stood up and charged at the monster but was stopped short by her wall of a hand. The girl tried to get around it but was easily herded back. "Where are they? If you killed my friend I will pull you apart!"

Marlite laughed. "You will pull *me* apart? Only if you were me, and I you."

"Where are they?" demanded Bonnie.

"Why? What are you? One of those mans?"

"Where are they?" she repeated, trying to get around the giantess's hand.

"Gone," said Marlite.

"Where?"

The giantess pointed to the Fire Sea. "There," she said.

"Jat went into the fire? He's . . . dead?" Bonnie leapt onto Marlite's hand and scurried up her arm. She dove at the giantess's face, poking a fist in her eye.

"Now, THAT hurt!" bellowed the holygiant, and she knocked the girl back to the sandy floor. Marlite rubbed her eye. "Stop this now! This giantess did not hurt your friend. This giantess helped them escape."

Bonnie stood back up, her balled fists hanging from taut, shaking arms. "If Jat went into that fire, he's dead. How is that helping him?"

"He helped himself, to say the truth of it. I helped Newton. They are together. If you stop trying to poke my eye, I will tell you where they went."

Bonnie relaxed her arms, but her fists remained clenched. Marlite explained what happened to the boy and the giant. When the holygiant finished, Bonnie ran up to the small teleoscope and searched the Fire Sea.

"You will not see them," said Marlite. "Newton's boots have carried them a fair distance by now."

"What if Jat turns back into a regular . . . person . . . while they're still in the fire?"

"He will burn? Mans burn, yes?"

"And it's clear you don't care."

"This holygiant has more to worry her than a squeaky mans pet." She sniffed the air. "And her biggest worry has arrived. You do not want to be here."

"Too late," said Bonnie. "I am. And I'm not afraid of giants."

"No, you are not," said Marlite. "I smell no fear in you. Do mans not know fear?"

"Mans do. But I'm not a man."

"Ha! This giantess sees what her friend saw in your kind. Stay here. Stay here or go out and die. It will change nothing for me." She took a few steps away and turned. "If you do not stay here, I cannot help you. And you will help no one inside a giant's gullet."

"I heard you," said Bonnie.

"I know, but this giantess feels you needed more warning."

Marlite left the house and walked up the beach. "I smell just one?" She turned toward the sound of crashing trees above the shore. Aphanfel stumbled forward, out of breath.

"Holygiant!" he said. "Where have you been? Where is Broont?"

"Gone," said the giantess. "Where are the others?"

Aphanfel clumped up to Marlite, eyeing her suspiciously. "Different places."

"*Different places* are as empty words. What is *different places?*"

"Flintoak is in the most different place—dead. Felled by something here. Crag and Greyelm are looking for a shrunken giant. Broont called them *mans.* It rode a skinny, long-faced ox. Crag thinks it will lead them to Broont. He thinks it rode back to where Flintoak fell."

"What killed Flintoak? What *can* kill a Flintoak?"

The spy shrugged. "Whatever it was, this giant is glad it is not him. Greyelm is in heavy squall. I did not want to be around him. And I think they are wrong. I think Broont came here. Did he? Is he?"

"Yes," said Marlite. "But no more. He escaped into the fire that brought us here."

"You let him go? How can a holygiant betray the Makers? We must find Crag and go after him!"

"This holygiant has decided to go after him. But not to bring him to Mother Shepherd. I am of a wish to help him find our . . . my once friend."

"Pryat is dead. You will be dead, too."

"That is not known to be of truth."

"What of the skyfire?"

"What of it?" asked Marlite. "Bend your back and look up. The skyfire is no more. The Makers' anger is no more."

Aphanfel hesitated.

"Well?"

"This giant finds uncomfort up there. It is too much . . . There may be no skyfire here, but here is not home."

"But here *is* home!" said the giantess. "We share a sky

with this land. Newton showed this to me. To punish a giant for a thing he has not done is of a great offense. Of as much an offense as letting a giant of guilt go free. Though Mother Shepherd may not share this thought, I believe it to be of truth. And I am here. She is not. Newton has not angered the Makers. If he has, they are no longer of that anger."

"Crag will not stop," said the spy. "He will not care if Broont is of an innocent way. He will not believe that skyfire no longer falls back home. Giants died to bring Broont back to our land. Crag will pull your bones from your hide for setting him free."

"I know he will try, Aphanfel. He is not a worry to this giantess. Greyelm? That is more of a worry. No matter. I will be gone when he returns."

"What will he do to me if I allow you to go?"

"If you *allow* me to go?"

Aphanfel was about to speak. Then he lowered his head. "This giant cannot stop you."

"Some words of truth from Aphanfel."

"But Crag will not care. This giant will pay for what you do."

"Good."

"They will follow you."

"Only to the floating trees. But they will find none there. I cannot have them following me to my friends. I have done them both great wrong, Aphanfel, as have you. And Mother Shepherd. Old Pegma . . . All giants! My boots will walk a thousand lifetimes until right is made right. I should have left with him!"

"And what of me? How will I get home? Can this giant join you?"

"HA! How could this holygiant trust Aphanfel the spy?"

"Aphanfel the spy will be Aphanfel the friend. Aphanfel the friend believes you. The Makers are not angry." He forced himself to steal a quick look up to the sky and then turned back to Marlite. "I will not harm a guiltless giant, Marlite. But to leave this one here is to take his life. Crag cares not for the *bond of word* that no giant will take the life of another. Think of Gossan! Let me help you instead."

"I need no help. I need no help from *you* even more."

"You will leave me to be thrumped by Crag and Greyelm then."

"*Oomph* . . . How can this giantess trust you?"

"How can you not trust a giant whose life you spared?"

"They will not blame you for me leaving."

"*Pffrump* . . . Do you believe this in truth, Marlite?"

Marlite stared into Aphanfel's eyes, appearing to search for something that either was or was not there. Then she sighed. "We go now, but . . ." Her braid shot out from behind her and wrapped around the spy's neck. Aphanfel dropped to his knees, eyes bulging in fear. Gurgling sounds bubbled from his grimacing mouth. He began to turn to stone. The holygiant released him.

"That was to remind you of your fate should this holygiant's trust in you grow weak."

Aphanfel got back to his feet and rubbed this throat. "You will not have to remind me again," he rasped.

"Now wait here. I have a thing to do."

Marlite took off toward Newton's house. Bonnie watched her from inside. The giantess tromped past her and barreled down the beach, hugging close to Newton's talking wall. The girl stepped outside and watched her shrink in the distance.

"Where is she going?" she asked herself.

The waves of the firetide rolled and slipped, slipped and rolled, rolled and slipped. A light evening fog wandered in from the forest and crackled in the flames. The ground began to pulse. Marlite was rushing back, the thump of her feet spraying sand in the air all the way back at the house. The girl ducked inside.

The giantess rejoined Aphanfel.

"Where did you go?" he asked.

"Not for you to know."

"What is that dust on your hands? It is blue. Do you bleed? Do holygiants bleed dust?"

"That is the most empty this giantess has ever seen a giant's head," said Marlite.

Suddenly, Trapper let out a snort back at the house.

"What is that?" asked Aphanfel, sniffing the air. "I smell it."

"I do not know," said Marlite. They tromped back toward the house and saw the horse. It paced restlessly by a window, bathed in the light from the glowing stone inside.

"The long-faced ox!" said Aphanfel. In three strides he was upon it. He picked it up and shoved it into his mouth.

"NOOOO!" shouted Bonnie, running out of the house. "TRAPPER!"

"The shrunken giant!" The spy bent down to pick up the girl. Marlite sent him flying with the back of her hand.

"It is the thing that killed Flintoak!" said Aphanfel, struggling to sit up.

"I didn't do it! Constable Stoggin did it! You just ate my horse, you . . ." She ran at the fallen giant but was stopped by Marlite.

"He won't let you do to him what this giantess let you do to her. We did not know it was your pet. Aphanfel owes you a balance in the take-give. He will make good."

"He . . . ate . . . TRAPPER!" shouted Bonnie. She picked up a rock and threw it at the giant. It bounced harmlessly off his forehead. "Go away! Both of you, go away!" She picked up another rock, aimed, and hit Aphanfel in the eye. The giant squawked and turned away.

"You have to watch your eyes with this one," said Marlite to the spy. She turned back to Bonnie. "We are leaving now."

"Just you? Where are the other giants?"

"Looking for you," said Aphanfel. "You made them angry. You make ME angry! They thought you went back to the place Flintoak was killed."

"They're what? You have to stop them!"

"We cannot," said Marlite. "I am setting out to find Newton. And your mans-friend." She pointed to Aphanfel. "This one is coming with me. My hope was to tell the other two giants to end their search. To return home. But they are not here. I do not know if they will even return. Maybe a Stoggin will thrump them, too. The longer we wait to catch Newton, the more steps there will be between us."

"But what about the mess you are leaving behind? What do we do to stop those giants from tearing our land apart? More than they already did! Our village is in pieces!"

Marlite thought a moment. She got down on one knee to bring her face closer to the girl's. "I do not know," she said. "And it washes this giantess in a bowl of sadness." Marlite pulled the vial of stoneturner oil from her robe and set it in the sand. "This may be of help. It turns a giant to stone. Find a way to get them to swallow it. A little will turn them for half a moon. More . . . will turn them forever. This holygiant does not wish that upon even them. But wishes often lose their way."

"Why do you do this?" asked Aphanfel. "We may need it."

"First we *trumple* the life of a giant. Then we *trumple* the lives of a herd of these *little giants*. We are of a need to do something right or a balance will never be made. *And* this giantess is fond of this little 'not-a-mans.'"

Bonnie stared at the huge vial. A look of fear grew on her face. "I don't know how I . . . I'm just a . . ."

"Nor does this one. But this holygiant smells a thing in you. It tells her that you will find a way."

The giantess stood. "We go now. You are wished a blessing of good fortune. But I fear your enemies may need it more." She walked toward the Fire Sea, her braid swishing back and forth across the sand. Aphanfel followed, head turned, looking down at the girl. Bonnie glared back up at him with a look that nearly made him shudder.

"I do not think I would want to eat that one," he said to the holygiant.

"I do not think you could," said Marlite, and the two giants stepped into the sea of flames.

TWENTY-SEVEN

Not a Nannytale

"What do we do now?" asked Jat.

"I do not know," said the giant through a mouthful of crabs. They were small but plentiful in the pools of water at the edge of the tide. "Do you think that dragon is of a concern?"

Jat laughed. "You're the giant. Is it? Can they eat you? That one looked big enough."

"This giant didn't know there *were* dragons. Maybe we should act as if it can eat us until we learn it will not." He crunched another handful.

"I think that's a good idea. We could go to the forest up there so we can have some cover. We're too easy to find out here. Especially you."

"Will there be more sandcrabs up there?"

"Probably not, so stuff your cheeks now." The giant took the boy's suggestion.

Newton and Jat walked along the base of the white cliffs. They searched for a break in the steep walls that led to the top. At last, they found a fissure wide enough to allow them to work their way up.

"Do you want to ride in my pocket?" asked Newton.

"No," said the boy. "I'm not a toy. I can climb."

When they reached the top they turned and looked out at the sea that had carried them here. Pale sunlight washed over the endless expanse of ice and milky-white water. *It looks so cold*, thought Newton, *yet it is so warm here on the shores.*

"We came a long way," said Jat.

"We have," said Newton. "I want to call out for Pryat, but I do not know if it would bring dragons."

"Or if your friend is even here. Can you smell him with that big nose of yours?"

"This *big* nose smells only trees. And a sweaty boy."

"You don't smell that great, either."

"Haroomph!"

"At least the trees are taller here than back at home. We're pretty well hidden from anything looking from the sky."

"Jat."

"What?"

"This giant is hungry."

"So is this man," said Jat. "I didn't eat, what, a thousand crabs like you did."

"We need to find food."

Jat thought a moment. "I'll go a little deeper into the forest to see if there is sign of any large animals. I want to get a better idea where we are, too. You wait here until I get back."

"Why should I wait here?"

"You're a noisy walker. If anything *is* here, it will run off long before you got there. And you're easier to see by whatever other things that might be here. There might be things besides dragons we don't want to be seen by. I know how to move quietly."

"What if something happens?" asked Newton, concerned for his friend.

"Somethings always happen. I'll be okay. Just a quick look around." Jat disappeared into the soft needles of the surrounding trees.

Newton sat and stared out at the water. *Is this home now?* He knew he'd never be able to make it back to his old home—either one of them. He was happy that Jat was with him, but he also felt bad that the boy would never see his family again. That he would not be able to keep his promise to Fira that he'd return. *That is my fault.* Pryat's fate was his fault, too. Everyone he cared about was worse off because they knew him—even his enemies. But whenever the guilt threatened to grow too strong inside him, he remembered what he'd done to cause all of this. *I looked up. I asked myself questions. I do not know how else to live.*

"Enough," he said to himself, slapping his thighs. "Cooking in my own regrets again." He reached up and pulled a seedcone from a tree. *Maybe this can be eaten?* They had similar trees back in his land, but the seeds were only eaten in times of hardship. He popped one in his mouth and bit down. *Sticky . . . bitter . . . but a thing to eat,* he thought. He had soon cleared the area of all the cones. It filled a little more of his belly, but he needed a good ox or goat.

Newton was beginning to worry about the boy, when the branches parted and he stumbled forward.

"Stupid roots," he said. "Tripped most of the way."

"And?"

Jat smiled. "You will be very happy. Very, very happy. Very, very, very—"

"Stop, boy," said Newton. "What did you find?"

"The ground drops down into a deep valley that is filled . . . with . . . deer! Or something that looks like them. Way in the distance, but now we at least know there's food here. They look pretty big, too. Bigger than the ones we have back home. Doesn't that make you very, very, very—"

"Show me," said the giant.

Jat took Newton to the lip of the valley. A great sea of swaying green grass lay before them. In the distance, they saw the dark shapes of what looked to be deer.

"I want one now," said Newton.

"I know. But hold on for just a moment. *Think*. If we walk across that valley, and a dragon happens to fly overhead, we will be seen. Again, especially you. I doubt there is just that one we saw. I would think dragons come from mother and father dragons. And there could be uncle and aunt dragons. Brother and sister dragons. There could be hundreds! Maybe we should stay here until tomorrow to see what shows up. If we see nothing, then maybe we can risk it. Can you make it that long?"

"Yes," said Newton. "And your caution is wise. It speaks louder than my grumbling belly."

"Nothing speaks louder than that."

They settled in for the approaching night. Both were asleep by dark, exhausted by their journey. At first light, Newton was awakened by a screeching roar. He sat up and looked across the valley. In the distance, dragons were swooping down and picking off the deer. A dozen or so circled above the herd, keeping it together in a tight pack so they could be easily captured. The giant watched, his mouth hanging open in awe. He turned and saw Jat, still sleeping on the ground. *Nothing wakes that boy.*

"Jat, wake up."

"*Ungh*... Not... yet," he mumbled, and rolled onto his other side.

"Dragons, Jat. Wake up."

Jat bolted upright and crawled to the edge of the canyon. "Those are... Blazes! All of those... Newton. There are lots of them!"

"Aunts and uncles and brothers and sisters."

"I'm sorry, Newton. I thought giants were pretty amazing, but next to dragons..."

"I would share that thought. This giant is grateful to you, Jat."

"For what?"

"For telling him to wait before going down there."

"I think we need a new plan. One that takes us in a *very* different direction," said the boy.

"Yes. We should go now while they are busy."

Newton took one more look at the hunting dragons.

This giant is no longer the biggest in the land. He turned back around to head into the forest and then froze. The giant let out a gasp and dropped to his hands and knees.

"What's wrong?" shouted Jat. "Are you all right?"

Newton stared at the base of the tree in front of him. He could not speak. He could not move.

"NEWTON! What happened?"

The giant pointed to the tree. Jat ran over to see what he was looking at. Lines were scratched into the bark. They looked like . . .

"Pryat?" asked the boy.

Newton sniffed the image. "Pryat!" he answered. "Pryat did this! It is him!" He sniffed again. "There is a very small smell of him, almost none at all, but some."

The giant felt as if his heart would burst in an explosion of joy. *My friend lives! He made it!* He gave the tree one more sniff. "It is old," said Newton.

"So he might not still be . . ."

"NO!" bellowed the giant. He stood and then bent down toward the boy. "DO NOT SAY IT! HE IS ALIVE!"

Jat took a few steps back. "Shh! Dragons. I'm sorry. Of course he is. But, um . . . I'm sure he is, but how do you know it's him? I thought you were the only giant that made pictures."

"Pryat has seen this giant's scratchings. First, he nearly turned to stone. But then he learned what they could do— what they could say. This," said Newton, pointing to the image, "is as what I showed him. Pryat knew this giant of all giants would understand."

"And I guess you smell him, too. On it. Okay. That's good!"

Newton turned back to the tree and embraced it in his massive arms. *You have made this giant grateful, Pryat.* He smiled. *And now* you *give* me *knots to untangle.*

"So which way do you think he went?" asked Jat.

"*Haroomph* . . . I do not know." He looked at the image again. It showed a giant, standing with his hands resting on his hips. A broad smile was etched in his face. "Look how he draws his arms bent at the elbow. It took me very long to figure that out—to bend arms and legs."

"Yeah. He's pretty good."

"We can't go across the valley, so maybe he thought the same."

"Maybe. We can go in the opposite direction, through the woods. It's the direction I'd want to go and it's the first thing that came to our mind. Maybe his, too. We have to assume he saw the dragons. But maybe he didn't. Maybe he . . ."

"No, Jat. Pryat knows how to keep the hide on his bones. He is smart in that way. We will go through the forest. Look for more of him on the trees. But first . . ."

Newton found a small rock with a pointed tip. He scratched an image of himself and Jat on the bark next to Pryat's drawing.

"Why did you do that?" asked Jat.

"If he comes back here, he will know his friends are look-ing for him." The giant put out his hand. "Shoulder. Not pocket, like a toy."

"What?"

"Ride on my shoulder. Yes, my boots make more noise than my friend Jat's, but my friend Jat's eat the trail more slowly. We must move fast to find him, and you cannot keep up."

"No, that's okay. I actually kind of like it up there. Just not the pocket thing." Jat hopped onto Newton's hand and was lifted to his shoulder. "It's good not having to shout, too."

"It would be easier for you, I know, if you had two hands to hold on."

"I have two hands," snapped the boy. He glanced over at the stone at the end of his wrist. "It's still a hand," he muttered.

Newton barreled through the trees. He traveled for days and traveled for nights, stopping only long enough for Jat to catch a bit of rest. The boy had rolled off his shoulder too many times, dead asleep. It was a far drop for a mans. *I should sneak him in my pocket so I can keep going.* Along the way they found bushes heavy with berries and trees laden with different fruits neither had seen before. Some tasted good. Some made Jat a little sick. Neither satisfied Newton's hunger for a very long time.

At each stop, Newton scratched a new image of Jat and himself on the side of a tree. Just in case . . . He moved with little effort, driven by hope, through a forest that grew taller, and darker. Occasionally, they'd see something moving above the treetops. Dragons maybe? It was hard to make them out through the leaves. He'd seen no new signs of Pryat. No scratchings. No smells. *But maybe no smells because of rains,* thought Newton. It had rained several times since they'd arrived.

The moon was a thin sliver when they'd set out. Now it was full. It was the same moon he'd always known. He could only see a piece of it, though, peeking through the treetop branches like flickering stars. *I am home wherever I can see you,* he said, his face straining to catch the light. The giant came to a stop.

"We can keep going, Newton. I don't think I need to stop tonight."

"No, this giant should rest, too." He sighed. "Your friend is tired of not being in one place. Tired of his boots carrying him from one land and then to another."

"Yeah. You have been doing that a lot."

"Just want to stop moving . . ." He lifted his hand to his shoulder. Jat climbed onto it and was placed on the ground. Newton dropped to the forest floor. *I do need rest,* he thought. *I don't want to ever get up from here.* The strength he felt at the onset had waned, sapped by the failure to find more clues leading to his friend. He began to fall asleep.

Jat circled around, stretching his legs. There was a small clearing ahead, one of the few they'd come across since they left what he called the "Valley of Dragons." In the middle stood a burnt tree stump. It sat awash in the moonlight streaming through the forest opening. "You know," said the boy, "if I were to leave someone a message, I couldn't think of a better place."

"*Poomfh* . . . Go have a look," said the giant sleepily.

Jat wobbled over to the stump. "My whole body is sore," he said. "You're a bumpy walker."

"So you have told this giant every ten steps. Shhh . . . sleep . . ."

The boy scrunched his eyes and studied the stump, walking around it. "Newton?"

"Shhh . . . What?"

"NEWTON?"

The giant sat up. "What? Is it . . . ?" He clambered over to the center of the clearing. "PRYAT! It is YOU!" He hugged the tree. "We found you! We *will* find you!"

"Did you see what he drew? Something's not right. Don't yell at me, but look at it."

Newton brought his face to the image. It was Pryat, but now his arms were in the air. *That is good, too*, thought the giant. *His arms bend AND lift! But what is that behind him?*

"Jat. Is that a . . ."

"Dragon. He drew a dragon. I don't know what that means."

Newton sniffed the stump. "This is still old, but less. Weeks less? But what is that other smell? Melted *glassss*? Do you smell it?"

"No, but . . . NEWTON! LOOK OUT!"

Jat saw it first, since he was already looking up at the giant. Newton felt the shadow that spilled over him. He scooped up the boy and dove to the edge of the clearing. The dragon floated down on quivering, outstretched wings. A sinuous neck snaked down to bring its scaly face level with Newton's. The giant looked into the golden eyes of the great winged creature. Newton began to feel sleepy. He tried to lift his feet, but he couldn't move. *It is doing this to me. It is like holy-giant magic.* The dragon's eyes went from gold to fiery red. It opened its mouth.

"Run, Jat."

"Can't."

A stream of flames washed over Newton's face and chest. The giant began to turn. *But why is there fear? They are only flames.* He smelled something burning. *It is not me. Is it my shirt?*

Newton leaned forward. "STOP!"

The dragon startled and pulled back its head. Then it let loose another torrent of flames.

"Are you still down there?" the giant called down to Jat. He was afraid to take his eyes off the creature.

"Nope," came a voice from the woods. "You may want to run, too."

Newton was starting to feel the heat, hot enough to burn an unburnable shirt. It was approaching the level of the Makers' Voice. "I SAID STOP!"

Once again, the dragon's mouth snapped shut. It tipped its head and gazed at the giant with a look of confusion. Newton lurched forward and wrapped his arms around the dragon's mouth, holding it closed.

"Stop! Please. Are you the dragon on that tree? With my friend—another giant?"

The beast struggled to pull free, but Newton held on tightly as he was lifted off his feet. Smoke began to pour from the dragon's nostrils as it gathered heat for another blast.

"No! Wait! Where is my . . ." A pair of hands grabbed the giant's ankles and yanked him to the ground. He landed hard, facedown. Newton rolled over and kicked blindly in the air. His foot caught the attacker's stomach.

"OOOPH!" it grunted, and doubled over. It was another giant. It was . . .

"Pryat?"

The other giant straightened up and looked at his old friend. "Newton?"

TWENTY-EIGHT

Old Friends and New

Pryat picked up his friend and squeezed him mightily in his arms.

"Cracking . . . my . . . bones . . ."

He let Newton down. "Sorry, my friend. You are here! You found me! How did you know where I went?"

"Some help from Marlite. Some help from you—your scratchings. They are very good! Your arms bend!"

Jat stepped into the clearing.

"What is that?"

"A mans," said Newton. "His name is Jat, and he has been of great help to me since I stepped out of the flames of the sea. He is this giant's friend."

"Did you know there's still a dragon sitting right there?" asked the boy.

"Elea," said Pryat to the dragon, "this is my friend. And his pet."

"NOT PET!" shouted Jat.

"No," added Newton. "Mans are as small giants. Or giants are as big mans. He is my friend just as Pryat is my friend."

The dragon bowed her head toward Newton and Jat.

"She thought you might be Crag. Or one of the others who went after you. I believed too many seasons had gone past for it to be you. Did they find you? What are you doing here? Newton, you are HERE! Where were you?"

"There will be time for tales of wandering giants, my friend. But know that this giant is well. Hungry, but well."

"And the Makers' Voice . . . ? Does it still . . ."

Newton smiled. "It is gone. *You* will smile when this giant tells you where it went."

"Your words find a welcome home in my ears," said Pryat. "This giant is well, too. And hungry."

"When were you not hungry?"

"HA! Once, but it was before . . ."

". . . you were born," finished Newton. "And probably . . ."

". . . not even then," laughed Pryat. "Has not a day passed since we were giantlings?"

"Many, Pryat. And too much has happened since those days. We are no longer those giantlings."

"Who would wish to be?"

"This giant . . . sometimes."

"So are dragons friendly?" asked Jat. "We were trying to stay clear of them."

"No, we are not," said Elea.

"You talk?"

"It helps to get one's *thoughtss* across, *mansss*."

"Elea is not as other dragons. She saved this giant from them," said Pryat. "And because of this, she is hunted by her kind. She saw you at the shore. I was of a thought it was not you but one of the giants who went after you. I was of a thought it would be best to not be found."

"This giant wishes you were NOT of that thought! It would have spared me another long journey in search of you!" Newton stood up straight and faced the dragon. He lowered his head and touched a fist to his chest. "My friendship is yours until the mountains turn to sand, Elea."

The dragon dipped her head. "May we fly that long."

"But the tree scratchings. They were for me, yes?" asked Newton.

"Oh, yes, but those are old. Before you came here. This giant was always of a hope you would find this place. As small of a hope as it was. And I knew the others would not know what to make of them. I was of a thought it might even scare them off."

"It brought me a great joy, Pryat."

"Come with us," said his old friend. "This giant yearns for tales of wandering giants. And your blundering friend has a few of his own."

Elea took to the air, and the three walked through the forest until they came to the edge of a deep ravine. The dragon was waiting. Two deer lay at her feet. Newton gasped. They were larger than a giant's oxes.

"Are those for . . ."

"A meal to pay for the *flamesss* I set upon you," said Elea.

They were gone in six swallows.

"One of those was for me, I thought," muttered Pryat.

"It is my regret," said Newton. His smiling face showed little regret, though. He felt a happiness he had not felt . . . ever. His belly was full. He had found his old friend. His new friend was safe beside him. And he now had a dragon bringing him food. Sated, he finally took in where he was.

The sun was just rising. Snow-topped mountains awash in gold, the gold of a dragon's eye, stretched on and on, growing paler in the distance. Sounds of waking birds rang in the valleys. Below, a wild river roared, loudly tumbling boulders of ice.

"This is where we stay now," said Pryat. "The sound of the river hides our own. Someday we will travel to the mountains. Elea says there are many different creatures there. This giant would like to meet them." He leaned toward Newton with a big grin. "Some sound like ridgebears!"

"When will you learn to stop getting thrumped by ridgebears?"

"When this giant stops getting thrumped by ridgebears."

"So we're safe from other dragons here?" asked Jat.

"We do poorly in the cold," said Elea. "Our wings *ssstiffen* and we cannot fly. This is the edge of our land. Few dragons come here."

"Yes," said Pryat. "We would have to *walk* to the mountains, since she cannot fly where there is snow. It will take a great span of time, but we have a wealth of it!"

"It is of great beauty here," said Newton. He filled his lungs with air and exhaled slowly. "In many ways."

"I am of that thought," said Pryat.

"Yeah, it's pretty good," said Jat.

"So where has my friend been since jumping into the sea?" asked Pryat.

"Let us sit," said Newton. He told of his journey across the Great Sea. Of spinning waters that carried him to the Fire Sea. Of new friends in the land of mans. Of skies free of skyfire. Of giants battled. Of the giantess who saved him. Of a journey with a little stone friend in his pocket. Of a sail that pulled two travelers across the white sea like seeds in the wind.

"You would be the most famous of giants if anyone knew where your boots have been," said Pryat.

"You know that is not a thing this giant wishes. No, Pryat. This giant has always wished to live as one unseen. Those who do not know about Newton cannot grow angry with him."

"I am pleased Marlite is Marlite again."

"Yes," sighed Newton. "Yes. Marlite is Marlite. But also, she is not . . . And now what of your story?"

"Another day, my friend. We will have many days. For as long as Elea is here, this giant will be here. And as she cannot leave, this is my home."

"Why can't you leave?" Jat asked the dragon.

"My wings will not carry me over a cold *sssea*. Pryat, I have told you more timess than even you should need to hear, 'Do not *ssstay* for me.' I did what I did for you because it was right. It was not my *desssire* to bind your fate to mine."

"But you did bind our fates, Elea. This giant is not wise like the one sitting there. He is not as powerful as the dragon who saved him . . ." Pryat looked down at Jat. "And he is not as . . . erm . . . *small? squeaky?* as this mans . . ."

Jat laughed. "Yup. That's me. Small and squeaky."

"But this giant is loyal. It is what makes Pryat, Pryat."

"I know this to be of truth, Elea," said Newton. "He is not going anywhere. The two of us together could not move him."

"And where would I go? *Why* would I go? Yes, dragons—*other* dragons—are a thing to be feared, but do not all lands have a thing to fear? Look at what happened in our own. Oh, and I do not really *fear* dragons."

Elea snorted. "Even a dragon would *hesssitate* to bite down on a big rock giant."

"Hush," scolded Pryat. "It was not this giant's proudest moment."

"I would stay, too, if I am welcome," said Newton.

Pryat smashed his fist into Newton's shoulder, knocking him onto his back. "Do you have *more* oafish words? Do you really think you would not be welcome?"

Newton sat up again, rubbing his shoulder. "This giant forgets that you do that . . ." Pryat smiled innocently. Newton continued. "There are walls for my stories. Sand for *glassss*. There are stones to build a furnace. And when my boots walk outside my head, there is a great sky above to welcome them. And a friend below to welcome him also." The giant stopped and looked down at the boy. "Oh. I cannot say this without knowing your wishes, Jat. You have been my guardian and friend since I left the Fire Sea. This giant is loyal to his friends, too."

"Okay, well, first, I've never felt so tiny in my life. And

second, when I am famous, and yes, *I* want to be, imagine what they will say about the man who was a friend to giants and dragons. But the real reason? Things seem to get better for me when I'm with you. And I think we're just getting started."

"So," asked Newton, "are we home?"

"Yes," said Jat. "We are home." He looked up at his friend and added a grin. "For now."

Newton laughed. "'For now' is good." The giant sighed and watched the last star of dawn fade into the morning light.

"For now" is of a good time to stop running—to be home . . .

· ACKNOWLEDGMENTS ·

It began with a frenetic flock of chickens coming to the rescue of a family of farmers. *Chickens to the Rescue* was my foot in
the door with Henry Holt & Co. and my introduction to a
remarkable woman who would play a very big role in my
career. Throughout the dozen or so picture books later, I have
had my editor Kate Farrell to thank for shepherding my stories through the briars, hills, and valleys of publication. She
saw something in this latest tale I had sent her—a story about
a curious giant—and worked with me to make it better so
others would see that something, too. It took a while, but she
got me there, ever patient, ever encouraging. For over a dozen
years I have benefitted from her gift of knowing how to draw
from an author his or her best. Every book I've done with
Holt has been a true and joyful collaboration with Kate.

Thank you, Kate, again!

When I asked my wife, Betsy, what she thought about me
taking a gamble to spend months (and months and months)
writing, to the exclusion of all else, a novel about a boy and
giant, she didn't hesitate. "Go for it!" she said. She always says
that. It's why I've been able to keep at this. Betsy continues to
have a faith in my career I sometimes lack. It is an invaluable
quality for which I am eternally grateful.

Thank you, Betsy, again!

My son, Jeff, is an artist. For years we have been trying to find a project we could work on together. His artwork has always blown me away, from his grade-school science-fiction drawings to today. Being an artist myself, I find it difficult to hand the illustration duties over to someone else. But I knew at the onset this one would be for him. I could not have done what he did with it. One of the biggest joys in my life was having him stay with us for two weeks while he created sketches for this book at our dining room table. It was he who figured out how a giant would actually use a *teleoscope*. He also has a keen ear for what makes a story work and provided some very key elements for this one.

Thank you, Jeff. Let's do this again!

In 2014 I started a critique group for children's book writers and illustrators in my hometown of Killingworth, Connecticut. A good number of these people are diving into an area that is new to them. This is not an easy thing to do. Their dedication and passion for the art is contagious, and they inspired me to push myself to try my hand at a new genre.

Thank you, my Thursday-night author/illustrator buddies! (We need a better name . . .)